The Legends of Regia

DARK SOUL

a novel

Tenaya Jayne

COLD FIRE PUBLISHING LLC

Other titles by Tenaya Jayne

Blue Aspen

Forbidden Forest

Forest Fire

Verdant

COLD FIRE PUBLISHING LLC

Copyright © 2015 Tenaya Jayne

ISBN-13: 978-0988275768
ISBN-10: 0988275767

Cover design by Cathleen Tarawhiti and Erika Doucesse

Edited by Amanda Fiske and Claire Ashgrove

Proofread by Ally Robertson

PROLOGUE

Regia, fifty years ago...

Years of combat in the royal army, stringent training for the Crimson Brotherhood, and seven medals celebrating Mycale's honor and bravery amounted to nothing with two katana in his back. The flames consuming his house lit up the night as the acrid smoke of burning wood and flesh filled his lungs. The screams of his life mate and children caused his body to jolt, adrenaline attempting to force his body to accomplish the impossible. As he struggled to get up, the blades were thrust deeper, pinning him to the ground.

Mycale had never failed in anything, ever. But now, he'd failed to protect that which he loved the most. His family died thirty feet in front of him while he lay powerless to save them. The screams of his son and daughter quieted, and he knew they were dead, but one moment before Geanna's life was extinguished, her voice cried out to him.

"Mycale! I love you!"

Then she was gone. She died before he could answer and tell her for the last time that he loved her. The spiritual bond of destined life mates crashed within him, utterly demolished. The light inside his heart turned black, the atriums and ventricles broke apart. He wanted to crawl into the flames and die beside them, where he belonged.

The blades impaling him slid back, removed from his torso. The rush of blood from his wounds soaked the ground beneath him. He attempted to pull himself forward to the house when a foot kicked him over on his back. The light of the fire moved along the length of the sword now pointing at his heart. Mycale looked up into the eyes of his best friend, Steven. And his broken heart broke a little more.

"Why?" Mycale rasped, his lungs full of smoke and blood.

The lifeless expression on Steven's face flinched, smoothed out again, and then crumpled completely.

"I'm so sorry. I'm just following orders." Steven's voice broke, and he looked up at the burning house, tears running through the soot on his face. "The wolves will be blamed for this, and the entire peace treaty will be forgotten."

"Geanna...the children... How could you?"

Steven closed his eyes and shook his head. "I'm sorry."

Steven stood directly over him, the hilt of his sword clasped in both hands. He lifted the blade over Mycale and plunged it into his chest.

****

The deaths of Mycale and his family was the catalyst to end the fragile diplomacy that had been formed between the werewolves and vampires. And it worked, the treaty died. Mycale, however, did not. The sword through the chest missed his heart by a breath. Hours later, lying half-dead next to the pile of ash that used to be his home, a werewolf on the run tripped over him.

Tek clambered to his feet, cursing whatever obstacle had tripped him and was immediately shocked from his thoughts of running as he surveyed the macabre scene in front of him. He crouched down beside the body at his feet and felt for a pulse. The light thump of the vein beneath his finger had him cursing again. Taking a deep breath, he grabbed the vampire by the arm and hefted him over his shoulder.

Tek labored under the dead weight. The constant flow of obscenities running through his head was directed at his mother's memory for teaching him to always help those in need, friend, stranger, or foe alike.

The pale sun broke the horizon and seemed to taunt him. He wheezed under his new burden, a nasty cramp in his leg and a shooting pain under one shoulder. He couldn't continue on in broad daylight with a charred heap of vampire across his shoulders, despite the fact he was traveling off the road.

He looked around. He had no idea where he was. The distant sounds of civilization made him apprehensive and hungry at the same time. Unloading the man on his back to the ground, he began scouting a place to hold up for the day.

An hour later, he was cursing his mother's memory again as he dragged the unconscious vampire into the obliging cave he'd discovered. Propping him against the moist rock wall, Tek did something he'd never done or even thought about before: he placed his forearm against the lips of a vampire. Still unconscious, the vampire opened his mouth and bit down.

Three gulps, and the vampire's crusted, bloodshot eyes sprang open. He watched as the vampire threw himself back, clutching and beating at his chest.

"NO!!" His cry of agony resounded off the walls.

Tek grabbed the young man by the forearms and had his seized in return. The vampire's eyes locked onto his again. Tek was no stranger to suffering, his own and that of others, but these eyes burned with the torture of the damned to a level he had never seen.

"You saved my life?" he demanded.

"Yeah, I did... And I can tell, you're not about to thank me for it."

Tek let go and tried to back up. The devil in those eyes wanted his blood, and not just for a light snack.

The vampire grabbed at his sides but found only empty sheaths, his weapons gone. His eyes shot back to Tek. "I'd appreciate it if you'd kill me now."

Tek blinked. "Aren't you polite."

"Just lend me a weapon, I'll do it myself."

"I'm sorry. Unfortunately, I'm completely unarmed."

The vampire got to his feet and looked out from the entrance of the cave. "Where are we?"

"No idea," Tek answered. "I left my last dwelling with the thought *anywhere but here.*"

The vampire turned. "Why did you save my life?"

Tek shrugged. "Morality. It's a serious flaw... You're a royal soldier?" He'd just noticed the embossed emblem on the scorched, damaged breastplate.

The vampire blinked confusedly for a second before looking down at his chest. His hands touched the holes through the metal. The next second, he was ripping the armor from his body. Tek backed away from him as he caught the look in his eyes again. How could eyes go dead and still burn like that?

He watched from the mouth of the cave as the burned soldier limped off a ways and began to bury his armor in the ground under a tree. He saved only a ragged scrap and used its sharp edge to carve into the tree trunk. Tek turned away from the sight as the vampire's grief began to pour out of him. He knew unquestioningly that crossing his path, into the middle of this terrible crime and the pain resulting from it, would change his already complicated life. He just couldn't yet see how.

Tek came back to the cave's opening at the sound of uneven footfalls. "I wasn't sure you'd come back."

"Neither was I," the soldier conceded, turning the rough scrap of metal over and over in his hand. "I must disappear...I must bide my time..."

Tek smiled ruefully. "Me too."

"I won't thank you for saving my life. As far as I'm concerned, I died last night with my family... But my body is still animated for one purpose... revenge."

Tek ran his hands through his hair and sighed. "I don't know where I'm going, or when I'll stop, but you're welcome to come with me, provided you don't slow me down."

The vampire turned his dark eyes to the ground, one hand rubbing a spot on his back. "I didn't heal completely, and after this amount of time, it means I never will. I'll probably always limp, but I'm still strong and well trained. I could watch your back."

"Okay." Tek extended his hand. The vampire caught it firmly and held fast. "My name's Tek. What's yours?"

Hesitation filled the vampire's face.

"I'll use any name you give me," Tek prompted. "Pick a new one."

The vampire nodded, hesitating again. "Merick. Call me Merick."

CHAPTER ONE

Unseen. That was how she lived, not one single soul had laid eyes on her in over a year. Solitary, she kept to the wilds and retreated whenever anyone wandered too close. She talked to no one except herself and sadly found her own company distasteful. High on a great precipice, she looked out over the world and could see all the way to the rose-colored Crystalline Sea, the setting sunlight glinting off its jagged waves. She sighed deeply at the approaching, desolate night. Lonely and bored to the point of unqualified despair, Netriet ran her fingertip along the sharp edge of the rock she'd found earlier. Its flinty weight felt rough and dirty in her palm. She contemplated the edge and what she could do with it.

Will you please stop trying to kill yourself?

"I would if you'd go away."

We both know I can't do that.

"I promise not to try to kill myself for the rest of today if you shut up and not say another word."

The shadow was silent for one minute before she began to hum a disjointed tune in the back of Netriet's mind. Netriet took a deep breath, trying not to give in to the tears of defeat layering under her eyelids. If only it could just be over, but the shadow never let her harm herself. When she focused on benign or pleasant things, the shadow would be quiet and retreat to the corners. But before long, before Netriet could really relax and breathe peacefully, the shadow's sharp fingers would start to scratch and pick at her tendency for negativity, prod deeply at her fear, and tickle the longing for revenge.

Sometimes she fought it. Sometimes she won. But when her defenses were down, the shadow would wrap its arms around her and whisper in her ear, skillfully seducing her into submission. Netriet hated her own weakness. The blackness of her scars and the dark tendril that circled her left eye bespoke of the disease within. She ached to get back at the persons responsible for all of her trouble... The elf woman who first put the collar on her hand and sent her to Philippe. She was the catalyst. And the transparent being in the Wolf's Wood who prevented her from dying and placed the shadow within her. Netriet didn't even know their names, but their faces were forever branded in her mind.

You want revenge, don't you?

"Shut up."

Why do you keep us out here away from everyone else? You'll never get your revenge like this.

"I'll never get revenge regardless."

Netriet looked down on the rising smoke of civilization as the closest town built their evening fires. A sharp-toothed wind picked up around her, sliding through her threadbare clothes, biting at her skin. She huddled down against a large tree trunk, wrapping her arm across her knees. How long could she go on like this? She often desired food but since her transformation, no longer needed it to survive. She existed with no purpose and no prospects, an entirely pointless entity.

Let's go back. The shadow crooned in its most seductive tone. *You're so lonely. I know you'd like to see your friends again. Huh? Forest? The ogre lady, Martia? She said she wanted you to come back. You never did. That was rude of you.*

Netriet sighed and shook her head. "I can't. I won't let you hurt anyone."

I wouldn't! I promise. Why do you think I'm so bad? I save your life almost every day.

Netriet ground her teeth. "You don't care about me. You're just afraid if I die, so will you."

Not true. I care about you. That's why I want you to go back. You've been through so much. I want you to have some happiness. Otherwise, why would I tell you to go see Forest? I hate Forest. But I'll suffer her company because you like her.

When Netriet made no more reply, the shadow fell silent for a while. Sleepiness came upon her.

You're cold... So, so cold...wouldn't you like to have your shawl back? The one you lost? You know where you lost it. We could go find it. You wouldn't have to see anyone if you didn't want to... Remember how beautiful it was? Remember how sweet it smelled?

Weary, frustrated tears slid down her dirty cheeks.

Admit it. You want it back.

"Of course I want it back," Netriet hissed. "I admit it. Happy now?"

The shadow said nothing. Netriet waited. Nothing. Damn it. The shadow had baited her successfully. The memory of the patchwork shawl twisted through her like the pain of a loved one's death. And with the image dancing in her mind, she felt a ravenous desire to hold it again. The shadow was right; she did know where she'd lost it. If luck was with her, she could find it in the moonlight and be back to the safety of seclusion before the next morning's sun reached its pinnacle.

Netriet stood and headed off into the darkening shadows of the thick wilderness. She walked at a steady pace, ever vigilant and aware of her surroundings so as not to be caught off guard by a stranger. The darkness bothered Netriet, but the shadow reveled in it, guiding her through effortlessly. The faces of people she cared for shimmered in her mind. Netriet abruptly dug in her heels.

"No. I've changed my mind. I'm going back."

Are not.

The shadow moved under her skin like oil and shoved her forward from within. Netriet stumbled as her feet picked themselves up and down against her will.

11

Look around you. You've never gone that far away from where you really want to be.

The shadow was right. She hadn't moved far past the Fair, or from Forest's land. She'd wandered in vast looping circles, but the Fair and the hope of acceptance there had remained the unacknowledged axis of her world. She marched on, unnaturally strong, her body never tired. The sight from her dark eye sliced through the night easily.

As she came close to the outskirts of Forest's land, a headache began vibrating deep in her skull, and she unconsciously started backtracking. She shook herself as her marvelous sight made out the edges of an invisible barrier, like a huge dome of energy. She reached out her hand and walked forward, experimenting. She couldn't touch it. There was nothing tangible to touch, but the magic there held her off like a magnet pushing away.

Netriet's face was caught between a smile and a grimace. There was no way she could cross onto Forest's land now. What had happened to cause Forest to need so much security? She continued walking along the edge of the protected barrier, coming close to where she'd been chased by two werewolves, where she lost her shawl. Her memories of that night came back into sharp focus. Any signs of the struggle were long gone. She walked along, her eyes searching for the brightly colored fabric, and abruptly everything in the terrain changed from the way she'd remembered it. So much so that she questioned if she had somehow lost her way.

The Fair had moved, not away but out, expanding. What she saw in the distance hardly resembled her memories. The evidence of construction was everywhere. Trees cut and cleared, a partial wall in the early stages of erection circled the extended parameter, and little houses replaced many of the colored tents. The ragtag camp was becoming a town.

Netriet approached quietly, continuing to keep an eye out for her shawl, but her attention was caught on what the people of the Fair had done, wishing she knew the answer as to why? The area of the wall obviously designated as the entrance propped up a dozing werewolf, fudging his guard duty. She laughed internally. Anyone taller than a child could easily get over the under-construction wall. In fact…that was exactly how she intended to get in.

****

Forest hunched over the lengthy report on her desk and pinched her tired, stingy eyes shut for a moment. She knew one couldn't throw centuries-old traditions of a world into the fire without there being some hang ups. The knowledge, however, hadn't stopped her from wishing. Just when she felt Regia was making progress toward unity of the races, some new whack job popped up and began stoking the dying embers of prejudice and hate. All the whispers were conflicted, and the new group was skilled at instilling fear. Of all the things Forest had anticipated facing in her first year as Hailemarris, a group of terrorists, wasn't one.

She pushed back from the desk, suddenly aware she was totally alone. Forest swore, realizing she'd lost track of time and would be home late, *again*. If she didn't get home in the next few minutes, Syrus would start to worry. She rolled the papers up and tucked them under her arm before closing up her office. Kindel and Ena must have gone home for the night hours ago. As soon as the door was locked, the magic protecting it pulled together over the entry.

Forest yawned as she strode out into the foyer, the heels of her boots clacking loudly on the stone floor. She turned the ring she'd made from her End of the Bridge around her finger so the silvery ball rested in her palm, about to send herself home.

"Goodni…" her farewell to the security ogres trailed off as she noticed there were none.

Her sleepiness vanished instantly as she turned around, her hand on the hilt of her sword. She was alone, or seemingly.

"Hello?" She waited a beat. "Security?"

Adrenaline poured into her stomach as a whispered laugh echoed around the room. She drew her sword as a figure stepped out from behind a column across the room. The young woman wore a green hooded cape and an expression of amused insolence on her pixie-like face.

"Madam Hailemarris, I presume?" She thrust her hands out with a flourish as she gave a theatrical bow.

"Who wants to know?" Forest demanded.

The young woman tsked. "We've been watching you. You're quite the crusader, aren't you? A real idealist trying to make a difference."

"I assume I've stepped on your toes in some way. Put a family member of yours away? And you're here for revenge, or you want a favor and have brought a bribe?"

"Oh, no. No bribe. As I said, we've been watching you. And apparently, you can't be bought."

Forest curled her lip at the young woman. "That's right. So what do you want?"

The young woman sighed and pulled a crossbow from her cloak, training the sight on Forest. Forest eyed the weapon for a second before sneering contemptuously.

"Apparently, you haven't been watching me for very long if you think that toy in your hands can subdue me."

"Not scared?"

"Not in the least."

The girl shrugged and dropped the crossbow. "I guess I wasn't the right choice as messenger."

"Deliver your damn message and be done with it. I want my dinner."

The girl brought her foot down on the crossbow. The arrow shot across the room toward Forest's feet. She moved to the side, but the arrow pulled a line behind it like a harpoon, and the tip was hooked not pointed. The cord hit Forest's ankle, the end swung around and dug into the leather of her boot before retracting backward, pulling her off her feet.

She managed not to crack her head on the floor, coming down hard on her elbow instead. She cut the cord with her sword and scrambled to her feet, her eyes darting around. The girl had vanished. Laughter echoed around the room again.

"Now that I've taken your ego down a notch, maybe you'll give me a little more respect."

The girl strode back out from the shadows.

"Clearly, you're here for games, but I'm in no mood to play."

The girl laughed, her voice changing into a deep baritone as she shifted into a tall werewolf. Shock and disbelief filled Forest. She'd never seen or heard of a shifter that could shift into the opposite sex.

"You'll play if I say so," it said.

"Who are you?"

A twisted smile broke over the big ugly face. "I like how you're using your manners now. I am Shreve, captain of the Aluka circle."

Rage began a controlled boil in Forest's head. "The insurgents."

"I don't care for that term, myself. We prefer to be called—"

"I don't give a damn what you want to be called. I'm placing you under arrest."

"Really? You and who else?"

Forest advanced on the shifter. It slunk to the side and began to circle, shifting again into a beast form, its arms elongating and its mouth stretching over pointed teeth as a snout protruded.

"You can't win," it slurred. The beast's mouth was now shaped only for tearing flesh, not talking.

"I'm a shifter too. Just because you look like a werewolf doesn't mean you're strong like one."

Shreve lifted a heavy arm into the air and brought his fist down on the floor, the stone breaking under the force of the blow.

Forest lifted one eyebrow, trying to conceal her surprise. "Okay, so you're a freak. But then you must know, so am I."

She threw her sword down and disappeared, using her elfish ability. Shreve's eyes darted around as he moved forward. His nostrils flared in an attempt to sniff her out. She moved behind him, grabbing a stone bust of late king Leramiun off its stand and throwing it like a football into the back of his head. He stumbled and went down on one knee. She ran up his back, digging her heels into his flesh as she launched herself off his shoulders back toward her sword. She rolled as she hit the floor, grabbing her sword. Dropping her invisibility, she faced him as he got to his feet.

She charged him head on, slashing a deep gash across the chest and spinning quickly away as he swung his huge arm at her. He roared, slashing at her with long talons that ripped through the back of her shirt. Forest jumped over a sweeping strike meant to knock her feet out from under her and sliced another line on the side of his neck. He sank back to one knee, trying to hold back the blood gushing from his wounds.

She brandished her bloodied blade at Shreve, who cowered backward. "You're under arrest."

Shreve's hand shot out, the talons shifting into long elf fingers as they grasped Forest's wrist. Shreve stood upright now in the form of a male elf with the signature red eyes of the *Rune-dy*, pushing down on the pulse in her wrist as his wounds mended before her eyes. She stood face to face with him, her arms going limp, as his eyes drilled into hers, scattering her thoughts, making her sleepy. He took her sword easily from her hand.

"Look at you, so easily hypnotized. Maybe Copernicus was wrong about your power. No matter, you're the leverage we need."

He hooked the blade under the chain of her Hailemarris necklace. The light flashed off the metal into Forest's eyes, breaking his mental grasp on her. She blinked, twisting her ring back into her palm, and thought of home as she grabbed at her sword, trying to take it with her as the End of the Bridge pulled her through the black portal to safety.

She landed on her hands and knees in her garden, without her sword, and a slice on her hand.

Syrus instantly grasped her shoulders and picked her up, holding her against his chest. "What just happened? I was making dinner, and I got the terrible sensation you were in danger. I was about to go to your office. Are you all right?"

Forest clung to him, shaken to her core. "No. I'm not. I was just attacked in the foyer of Fortress by a… I don't know what."

Syrus hooked his arm under her knees, carried her into the house, and set her down on the couch. "Now, tell me."

"It was one of the insurgents, said its name was Shreve."

"*It?*"

"Yeah. I've never seen anything like it. At first, it was female then it shifted into a male. And when he shifted into a beast, he had the strength of a beast. I got the upper hand, about to arrest him, then he shifted into an elf, and he… mesmerized me, or something." She looked at her bleeding palm. "Shit. He got my sword. Hold on, I've got to call Redge."

Forest pulled her phone from her pocket and dialed Redge.

"What can I do for you, Forest?" he answered.

"I need you to get your team and go to Fortress. I was just attacked by one of the insurgents. They took out security. I had to use my portal to save my own neck; I wasn't able to check on them. I'm sure the insurgent is gone by now, but get any evidence you can. And be careful. I don't know exactly what we're up against here."

"Understood," he said sternly. "I'll report back as soon as it's done."

"Thanks, Redge."

Forest put her phone down on the coffee table and sighed. "Well, that was embarrassing."

"What was?" Syrus asked, looking at her palm.

"I just got my ass handed to me."

"I'm sure you got some licks in."

"A few, but..." She hissed in pain as Syrus shot a few red sparks from his fingertip into her wound, sealing it instantly. "You're really good at healing now."

"The new masters give me plenty of practice when they hack on each other during sparring," he chuckled, pressing a kiss onto the place he just healed.

Forest exhaled her stress. No matter what was happening, so long as she had Syrus, she was okay. She placed her hand on his cheek and looked into his grey eyes. She loved him more every passing day. He was her home, the stronghold for her heart.

"So, you made a new formidable friend, who took your sword. Did you learn anything else?"

"Yeah, he dropped the name Copernicus and said I was the leverage they needed."

Syrus went very still, the color draining from his face.

"What?" Forest asked.

"Damn it," he whispered, gathering her into his arms.

"What is it?"

"You don't know the name Copernicus?" he asked.

"It sort of rings a bell, but I don't know how."

"Let's hope, for all of our sakes, that the one now calling himself Copernicus is an imposter."

Chapter Two

Merick sighed and rolled on to his back, trying desperately to fall asleep. He stubbornly stared down insomnia, refusing to let it win. Insomnia just laughed in his face. The Fair had gone completely quiet, as it was now the tail end of the night with dawn just two hours away. He must be the only one awake with the exception of the night watchman. A frigid breeze blew through the flaps of his tent, the fabric sliding and slapping annoyingly.

Finally accepting it as a lost cause, he kicked his blanket off and rose to a sitting position. His trusty old cot groaned under his weight. In the last few months, Martia had been badgering him to upgrade his lifestyle, and he'd let her fuss over him as if she were his mother from time to time, but he resolutely clung to his rickety cot, insisting he didn't need a bigger or more comfortable bed. Cranky as he had been about everything becoming more permanent in the Fair, he couldn't deny the expanded room of his tent and the new solid frame made him more comfortable. It was silly to do more than he had though. Others needed comfort, not him.

Nevertheless, not for one second did he regret the dressing area he designated centric in his tent with its large stone bathtub next to the wood-burning chiminea he'd haggled away from Tek when the last goods caravan from Earth had come through. He wouldn't go so far as to run pipes to his tub; filling it by hand didn't take that long, and the stone held the heat of the water for hours.

Merick rubbed his head in little circles with his fingers and closed his eyes. She came to his mind as she often did at night... Nettie. He remembered her name, her haunted look, her strange eye, and her perfectly full lips. She bothered him the first and only time he'd seen her, and she lingered as no other woman had since Geanna died. He often wondered what had become of her. He'd even killed two werewolves to save her life.

Grabbing his pipe, he headed out into the cold night air. Maybe he'd go talk to whoever was on watch for a while. The cold caressed his back and slid into his flesh, striking at his old wound, bringing out the ache. He opened his mouth in a wide yawn only to choke on it the next second. A slight movement from the edge of the woods caught his peripheral vision. Holding himself perfectly still, he focused on the darkness.

And there she was.

He blinked, certain his eyes deceived him, but it was her... walking toward him as though she had just stepped out of the mists of his dreams.

He watched her eyes drift along the wall as she approached silently. She stopped, a small gasp escaping her mouth as she locked her gaze on him. Merick lifted his hand and gestured for her to continue her approach. She hesitated, her eyes darting around quickly before she took a small step forward. She looked wild, feral. After another moment of hesitation, she moved forward to the edge of the wall and stopped.

"Hello." Her quiet greeting shattered any notion he had that she was a hallucination.

"What are *you* doing here?"

A scowl pulled across her face. "Ah, yes. I remember you. The rude juggler."

Merick scowled back, annoyed he'd made such a bad first impression. "That's right. And I remember you, Nettie."

She cocked her head to the side. "You remembered my name. I'm not sure if that's sad, creepy, or..."

Merick's scowl turned more sour as she groped for another insulting word. "Or what?" he demanded.

She blinked at him a few times. "I was going to say nice, but I've changed my mind."

He narrowed his eyes. She pursed her lips together, and then, to his amazement, she giggled.

"What's so funny?"

"You. I think I read you wrong before. You're harmless, all bark and no bite."

Merick felt his mouth fall open. "*No bite*? Why don't you insult my manhood while you're at it?"

Her cheeks flushed, and she looked away from him. "Umm. I came here to see Martia… A lot has changed." She placed her hand on the wall and gave it a pat.

"Yeah, lots of change," he said tersely. "Here, I'll help you over."

She sneered and took a step back. "Don't touch me. I'll just go around to the front."

"Oh, great idea. You'll alarm the watchman, who'll overreact and wake everyone up." Merick cursed his tone of voice. Why couldn't he say anything right?

She sighed and looked back toward the woods. "This was a mistake. I shouldn't have come."

Panic ran up his spine as she turned and strode away.

"Wait. Please."

She stopped and glanced over her shoulder.

"Martia wants to see you. She's worried about you since you didn't come back that night."

"I'll come back later to see her. After everyone is awake."

Merick didn't believe her. He feared if she left now, he'd never see her again. She continued to walk away.

"You look terrible," he said hastily.

She stopped mid-stride and turned on her heel, marching back toward him, feminine fury burning in her eyes.

"*What?*" she hissed through clenched teeth.

"And you smell even worse."

Nettie's mouth fell open.

"Apparently, you haven't looked at yourself in a mirror or bathed in some time. Do you really want Martia or anyone else to see you looking like that?"

The angry defiance slipped from her face as she held her hand up and looked at the dirt. The next moment tears began to slide through the grime on her cheeks. Merick's heart buckled.

"I'm sorry. I shouldn't have said that...I stuck my foot in my mouth. It's not how I meant it to sound."

"Oh?" Her voice broke.

"Why don't you come into my tent? You can have a bath, and I'll find you something clean to wear. That's what I meant. I didn't want you to be embarrassed."

When she said nothing, he pushed on. "Besides, if you greet Martia looking like that, she'll fuss over you something awful. She'll lock you into her spare bedroom and force fattening food down your throat until she's satisfied. Trust me, you don't want that, she fusses over me all the time."

Nettie wiped her hand across her tears, smearing them like war paint.

Merick held out his hand to her. "Come on. I'll help you over this sorry excuse of a wall."

"Why do you want to help me?" She gave him a hard stare. "What are your ulterior motives?"

Merick was about to say he had no hidden motives, but he instinctually knew she wouldn't believe him. "I was hoping if you felt indebted to me…you might be persuaded to"—he fought not to laugh at the dirty look she was giving him— "persuaded to tell me how you lost your arm."

She took a step back, looking as though she was about to bolt again.

"I've got a great interest in people's old injuries, you see, as I have one myself."

"You do?" she asked.

Merick patted his lower back. "Yup. Took a couple of swords to the back once. Never walked right since." To prove it to her he walked in a little circle, demonstrating his limp. "Come on." He offered his hand again. "Come over."

This time, she gave him her hand.

****

Get us out of here.

"Shut up," Netriet hissed through her clenched teeth. She needed to learn to talk to the shadow without speaking aloud if she was going to be around people.

She could feel the shadow's panic. It was quite satisfying. She allowed herself to thoroughly enjoy the shadow's discomfort, knowing any second it would have enough and physically push her out of the tent and back to the wild.

"This was your idea. You're the one who wanted to get back to civilization," Netriet whispered.

I don't like him.

"Of course you don't."

Netriet fidgeted and looked around Merick's sparse bedroom. Minimalist, and worn down, but clean and smelled male, in a good way, not a sweaty foot kind of way. There was not one trace of a woman's presence. He clearly didn't have a lover.

The sound of water splashing made her jump and move to the flap of fabric that separated where she stood from the next room. Peeking through, she saw Merick pouring steaming hot water from a kettle into a grey stone tub. The immensity and beauty of the bathtub surprised her. Heat from the little, strange-shaped fireplace feathered pleasantly across her face. He was drawing her a bath. She had expected a wet rag and a leaky bucket of cold water when he'd offered to help her clean up.

He turned his dark eyes on her. She stared at him openly, unhurriedly, and he stared right back. There was one moment for Netriet...she didn't know what she felt, but she knew what she *didn't* feel. She didn't feel afraid. She didn't feel ugly. She didn't feel worthless.

The absence of the things she had felt for so long was like salve to a wound. His eyes held no judgment or pity. They were so dark, they were almost black, but they weren't cold. They were warm like a summer night. Understanding. How could she feel that? How could anyone have the smallest understanding of whom or *what* she was? She pulled her gaze away and looked at the floor, suddenly assaulted with the thought that he might be able to see what slithered behind the surface.

"Hey," he said quietly.

She looked up again.

"It's all right."

"What is?" she snapped.

"Everything."

She swallowed and blinked back the rogue tear pushing under her eyelid.

"This is ready for you," he said, gesturing to the bath. "I'm going to take a little walk, give you some privacy. There's some clean clothes in the chest at the end of my bed. Help yourself to whatever you can find that might not fall off you too badly."

She nodded. He opened his mouth and then shut it again, shaking his head.

"Thank you," she said to his back as he left.

He shrugged in acknowledgement and kept walking. Her clothes fell to pieces as she took them off, leaving her no choice but to wear his once she was clean. Sliding under the water felt alien and seeped sensual ecstasy down to her bones. Holding her breath, she sank all the way under the surface. Her heart thumped loudly in her ears, its rhythm amazingly easy and relaxed.

"You're unusually quiet," she said to the shadow as she came up for air. "Have you gone back to the stinking abyss I wish you into every day?"

Don't get your hopes up.

"*Hopes?* What are those? You've stolen any hopes I ever had."

The shadow tsked but said nothing else. Netriet inhaled sharply as she literally felt the shadow move. She braced herself for it to begin pushing her around…it didn't. It pulled away from her extremities and slunk back into a smaller point, and as best as Netriet could tell, was sulking. Netriet raised her hand to her mouth, touching the almost forgotten expression: a smile.

Being clean was the best sensation she'd experienced in such a long time that she couldn't find anything to rival it in her present memory.

The battered chest at the end of Merick's cot opened easily. Very worn, but clean clothes were folded on the top. She struggled to get the plain, bone-colored shirt over her head. It hung loosely on her shoulders and *barely* covered her butt. Her wet hair dripped onto the fabric, causing it to cling to her back. She looked through the chest for some pants, only feeling defeated when she found some. There was no way they would stay up, let alone allow her to walk; the legs would go past her toes.

Continuing to rummage, she unearthed a brightly colored quilt that was clearly Martia's handiwork. The sight of it smarted in her chest. She desperately wanted to find her shawl again. Under the quilt was a store of weapons, knives, and throwing stars embossed with the seal of the Crimson Brotherhood. It's none of my business, she thought, and kept looking for something she could cover her ass with. Loose coins covered the bottom of the chest—she tried hard not to be impressed with the amount. And seeing how Merick left this unlocked and told her to get things out of it, he clearly didn't care about his wealth. Either that, or he had so much more somewhere else this was nothing but disposable pocket change.

The sound of approaching footsteps had her panicking. There was nothing else for her to do but dive under the covers on the cot to make herself decent.

"Nettie? Can I come in now?"

"Yeah."

Merick ducked under the flap and stopped dead in his tracks. Netriet could feel her cheeks burning. She looked down to make sure her chest wasn't exposed in any way in the overly large shirt. On the verge of explaining why she was in his bed, Netriet found the words died in her throat at the expression on his face. He looked at her in such a way her heart clenched tight. They stared openly at each other, again. There was no doubt what was running through his mind, and knowing it only made the same thoughts run through hers.

How had she not noticed before? Well, she noticed now. Merick was gorgeous. His looks weren't flashy, but she had never seen a more perfectly featured face. Sure, he was older and a little damaged, but she saw strength, integrity, and warmth. A warmth she desperately craved. She imagined the warmth she'd feel if he wrapped his arms around her. Could he chase the darkness away?

****

There has to be another explanation for this…other than the one stuck in my head, he thought. *Surely, she's not offering?* He tried to capture his reason and keep a firm grip on it as he took in the scene. The lid on his chest was open, a pair of his pants lay on the ground, and she desperately clung to his blankets. *Okay, I think I see what…*but his thoughts went skittering in all directions, leaving him defenseless at the sight of her clean, flushed skin, her wide steady gaze, and her damp hair that caused the fabric of his shirt to cling.

"Merick?"

He felt as if he actually swallowed his Adams apple before answering. "Umm…Nothing fit too well?"

She shook her head.

"Okay, well, people are starting to wake up and move around, so I'll go see what I can find." He leaned over his chest and dug out a handful of coins.

She gasped. "Just to borrow right? Please don't purchase anything for me. I could never pay you back."

Merick chuckled. "The money is for me. I'm out of my pipe weed. Just stay here. I'll be back soon."

Nettie snorted. "Where would I go dressed in nothing but your shirt?"

He looked at her again for a moment before escaping into the morning air. Now he had no choice but to get a new bed. He'd never sleep peacefully in his cot again, not with the memory of how she looked under his blankets chiseled permanently into his head. No, he'd have no peace.

Merick kept his head down as he shuffled across the Fair to Renee's tiny, newly built structure she used as a storefront to sell clothes, fabric, and sparkly things girls liked. Peeking through the window, he could see her moving around in the back of the shop. He decided to go around the side and let himself in.

"Renee?"

The wizened old elf woman gave him a withering glare over her hunched shoulder. "I'm not open yet, Merick."

"Yeah, I know. Look, I need some clothes for a…friend of mine. She's about this big." He held his hands up to demonstrate how tall and broad Nettie was.

Renee croaked out a gritty laugh and turned her full attention on him. "Got a female friend who urgently needs some new clothes? HA! What happened to her old ones?"

Merick sighed. "They're lying in a torn heap on my bedroom floor."

Renee cackled again and gave him an approving thump on the shoulder. "Well, look around, but be quick about it. I'm about to open, and given the nervous sweat beading on your head, you don't want to be seen in here. Am I right?"

"Completely."

Merick scanned the room for a second then turned back to Renee. "Help me! All I see is piles. Where can I find something this size?" He demonstrated Nettie's height and girth again.

Renee smiled and hobbled over to a table laid with folded garments. "What colors does she like?"

"Not a clue."

"Is she tough or feminine?"

Merick shrugged.

Renee tsked and began holding things up for him to see. He grabbed a plain pair of black pants and was about go with that, figuring she could make do with his old shirt when Renee held up something that stopped him. The two-layered shirt had creamy sleeves and a quilted bodice of deep amber velvet just the color of Nettie's eyes.

"Yeah, that," Merick said.

"You might not like the price."

"I don't care. How long will it take you to alter it?"

"*Alter it?*"

"I'll pay you double your usual altering fee if you can remove the right sleeve and stich it closed."

She pursed her wrinkled lips. "Triple my fee, and I'll have it done in a few minutes."

"Ugh…fine. Triple."

Renee took the shirt and sat down. Merick paced the back of the shop while he waited. He was about to ask her how long it would actually take when she held up the finished shirt for his inspection and named the full price for the shirt, pants, and alterations. He dropped a handful of coins into her reedy palm. She smiled sideways up at him, pocketed the money, and wrapped the garments discreetly inside a brown remnant. She winked at him as she handed it over.

"You might want to work on your bedroom technique, Merick. A woman doesn't take kindly to such wardrobe abuse."

He scowled at her and dropped a few more coins into her hand. "For your silence."

"Don't insult me, boy. I know things about the people in this Fair that would shrink your fangs. I don't gossip."

He shrugged and held his hand out for her to give his money back. She quickly slid the money into her pocket and smiled.

"You're a good tipper, Merick. Thank you."

"Maybe I'll go to your competitor next time."

"The hell you will," she growled, pushing him out the side door and slamming it behind him.

No one he passed on his way back to his tent seemed to notice him. Everyone was still stuck in morning grogginess.

"Hey, Nettie, I found something for you to..." His words trailed off as he entered his tent. She was snuggled down in his cot, fast asleep.

He approached slowly, listening to her breathing. She was deep. He laid the clothes on the foot of the bed and left. The temptation to stare, touch, and fantasize was too heavy. He had to leave her alone.

Merick rubbed his head, bemused. What was he doing? What did he want from her? What did he expect? Why did he hide the pack and shawl he knew was hers instead of just giving it to her? He couldn't answer the last question and didn't want to acknowledge the answers to the others. He shoved his hands into his pockets and stalked off to see if Martia would feed him breakfast.

CHAPTER THREE

Baal sat perfectly still, the picture of attentive interest, while his insides churned painfully. The fact that he was merely an assistant and his opinion was not worth as much as the other priests usually annoyed him, but today he was thankful. No one noticed his discomfort and thus didn't inquire about its nature or origin. He wasn't listening to what Rahaxeris was saying. Panic began centering on the boils around his ribs as one of them broke open and stinging poison lazily ran down his side.

"Baal?"

"Yes, sir?"

"What do you think?" Rahaxeris asked.

"Umm…I agree with Menjel."

Rahaxeris raised one eyebrow, a faint trace of annoyance on his face. "Very well. You and Menjel are still out-voted, however. Hezeron and I shall depart tomorrow for the new world to extend diplomacy and glean what we can about the people and society. Menjel shall act as high priest in my absence. Everything else shall continue as usual. Keep up on your experiments. Baal, you shall spend a minimum of one day a week at Fortress doing whatever Forest needs you to do. Understood?"

"Yes, sir."

"Anything else?" Rahaxeris asked the room in general.

No one said anything.

"Very well, meeting adjourned."

Menjel gave Baal a meaningful glare, but he didn't have time to talk now. More of his boils had broken open, and the toxic fluid burned his skin. He rushed to his personal chambers as quickly as he could without running. Menjel would be knocking down his door in a moment.

Baal stripped off his priest robe and threw it over the back of his chair. His undershirt stuck to his skin. He pulled gingerly at the fabric. That was a mistake he realized too late, hissing through his teeth in pain.

The knock at his door came faster than he expected.

"Baal, we need to talk," Menjel demanded.

Knowing he wouldn't wait but a few seconds before letting himself in, Baal struck the wall and escaped through the portal. He landed on his feet and quickly closed the portal and did his best to erase its trace so Menjel couldn't follow. He walked quickly through the wild, overgrown area to the edge of the Wolf's Wood and ducked inside the boundary.

The instant assault of negative energy swirled around him as it always did when he came here. He couldn't deny it was getting stronger, pushing against him uncomfortably. His more frequent visits must be bothering the wood's guardian.

"Yeah, I know you don't want me here," Baal said aloud to Shi.

She didn't answer, not that he expected her to; she never talked to him.

He made his way quickly through the trees to the hidden home of Maxcarion. The magical illusion protecting his front door was plain as day to Baal's eyes. He knocked urgently against the rock.

"Come on," Baal said, the burning pain was growing cold.

The rock face slid open as easily as a silk curtain. Maxcarion's magically protected home was stuffy and disorganized, filled with knickknacks both wondrous and highly dangerous. Baal hated the disorder.

Maxcarion sat in the corner in a rocking chair, his face obscured by a large book. He peeked at Baal over the top for a second before disappearing again behind it. "I told you it wouldn't work," Maxcarion said idly.

"You said nothing of the sort. I need you to reverse it."

"What did you bring me?"

"Nothing, I didn't have the time. I had to get out fast."

Maxcarion tsked.

"Come on, you know I'm good for it."

"Ha! Those boils must be addling your brain. I don't extend credit." He looked at Baal again over the book. "Those sores will spread. I wouldn't go out in public for a while if I was you."

"Fix it," Baal demanded coldly. "Or, I'll never come back again."

"What do I care?"

"Oh, you care. You'll have to come out of hiding to get your own toys. Oh wait, you're too scared to come out. And who else can help you regain your full power and immortality? None of the other *Rune-dy* will help you. Rahaxeris is strong enough now to kill you, and Menjel would run experiments on you. You need me."

"Who are you trying to convince?" Maxcarion asked, closing his book.

They both tried to stare the other down. After a moment, Maxcarion sighed and crossed his arms across his chest. "You owe me one, unflawed Talereneain artifact."

"What?! Unflawed?"

Maxcarion shrugged and picked his book back up. "Like I said, those boils will get worse before they get better, *if* they get better. Maybe next time you'll take my advice and not experiment on yourself."

Baal hesitated a moment. Another boil burst. He braced his hand on the nearest table as his breath came out in short gasps. "All right! I'll get you the artifact. Just reverse this!"

"One moment... Let me finish reading this page."

Baal ground his teeth together.

"All right, let's see," Maxcarion said, setting his book aside and getting to his feet.

He grabbed Baal's hand and felt his pulse with an age-gnarled finger. Then he looked closely at his eyes.

"It was a good idea, but your DNA isn't compatible with the protein. Might I suggest you try magical means in the future and abandon science?"

Baal raised an eyebrow. "No I...I need both. That's it! I need to use both."

"Here, drink this." Maxcarion pressed a bottle of blue liquid into Baal's hand. "It won't taste good."

"When does it ever?" he retorted, tossing the blue stuff back. He shivered with revulsion at the taste as it slid down his throat. Small puffs of smoke hissed from his open boils before his flesh healed. Baal pulled his shirt over his head and ran his hands over his healed skin, exhaling with relief when he saw there were no scars.

"I don't know where you think I'm going to get an undamaged Talereneain artifact," Baal demanded.

"You might try the Fair."

"The what?"

"The Fair, that little disheveled excuse of a community."

"Why would I ever stoop so low to show my face there?"

"They are about to have their annual bazaar. Merchants and traders from all over Regia come to peddle goods. Most of them don't know their heads from a hole in the ground. You'd be surprised at the treasure that slips unwittingly through their fingers. If they have anything of real value, they'd never know it. Trust me, it's worth a look. You might find my artifact, or something of equal value I might want."

"Hmm..."

"Is there anything else? If not, I'd appreciate it if you'd leave me to my reading." Maxcarion sat back down and disappeared again behind his book.

Baal looked around the cramped space as he had many times. He picked up the collar sitting on top of a small table and rolled it between his thumb and forefinger. "When are you going to lower your price for this to something reasonable?"

Maxcarion looked over the rim of his book, made a little grunt in the back of his throat, and went on reading.

Baal reluctantly set the collar down. One day, he'd have it. Bundling his soiled shirt in his hand, he left. The negative energy of Shi sparked around him as soon as he stepped out into the open air, as if she were trying to shove him out.

"Yeah, yeah, I'm leaving."

He contemplated going back to *Rune-dy* headquarters or going home. If he went back to headquarters, he'd have to listen to Menjel... home it was. The force of his power concentrated in his hand before he struck the air, opening a portal.

The blissful silence of home wrapped around him as his feet hit the ground again. He looked around the heavily wooded area for traces of snoops or wanderers. The only footprints were his own from when he'd left that morning. He walked next to the base of the cliff, ducking under the sharp tree branches. The cold of the stone reached out and clawed at his bare shoulder. Reaching his disguised front door, he ran his hand over the rough rock, inlaid with runes. It wasn't as smooth or hidden as Maxcarion's home, but he was proud of the illusion he'd created. The stone ground against itself as it opened to him.

****

Shreve shifted into a small-framed male with weak arms and limp wrists, as a show of submission, before bowing low in front of Copernicus. "I am sorry, Father. Forest was able to open her own portal and escape my grasp. I'm not sure how she did it. Do you think, perhaps, Rahaxeris has taught her to—"

"I don't think so, but more information is needed before I can answer that question," Copernicus said in a low, controlled tone.

"She is not like you and me, as you once suspected. She is only an elf, shifter hybrid. Rahaxeris' natural daughter."

"Hmm..." Copernicus crossed his arms over his chest and looked away from Shreve, brooding. "Natural daughter," he repeated in a whisper. "It doesn't matter...in fact, it gives her more power... strengthens our plan. Did you learn anything else?"

"Yes, Father. I got her sword. I believe she is quite attached to it." Shreve held Forest's sword out for Copernicus, who took it by the hilt.

He swung it once to test the balance before running his finger along the edge, drawing a line of blood. Copernicus sucked at his cut finger before chuckling. "Beautiful artistry. Silver. Little sister doesn't like vampires."

"Not so, or not anymore. I've since learned she's mated to vampire. A powerful mage."

"Interesting. How powerful?"

"The most powerful in all of Regia. They call him The Sanguine."

"Well, that's a problem, isn't it? And since you were unable to apprehend her, her mate will be on the defensive."

"Are you going to punish me, Father?"

"Of course, but not now. I don't want to weaken you right now. It can wait until you bring Forest to me."

"Yes, Father. Thank you."

"Are there any new recruits?"

"Two. An older female shifter and a young male vampire."

Copernicus sighed and got to his feet, gesturing that Shreve should rise from his bow. Even after Shreve returned to his more natural muscular girth and height, Copernicus still stood a head taller than he did.

"Bring them in."

Shreve left the room. Copernicus sat back down in his high backed chair in the center of the otherwise empty room. It was a makeshift throne room. Soon, he would sit on the real throne in the Onyx Castle. Debts of the past would be paid to him. All the power of Regia he would take as his birthright.

A moment later, Shreve came back with the two newbies.

"May you live forever, King Copernicus!" the vampire said passionately, going down on one knee.

The woman made no such display. Instead, she scowled and crossed her arms over her chest.

"Why are you here?" Copernicus demanded of her.

"I, uh…heard about the circle from a friend of mine. They said you were a shifter."

"Outrageous!" the kneeling vamp said. "He's a vampire. He's going to claim the vampire throne."

Copernicus stood. "You're both right. And you're both wrong."

"So you're not a vampire?" the woman asked.

Copernicus walked up to her and pinned both her hands behind her, bringing his face close to hers and showing his fangs. "I am everything. Vampire, werewolf, ogre, shifter, and elf. All that Regia is lives in me. I am this world's heir, and I will claim my throne. Now join me or die."

The woman shook with fear but nodded. Copernicus cut his fingertip on the edge of one of his incisors before plunging his fangs into the side of her neck. She screamed. He pulled back and stuck his bleeding finger into the bite mark, making her his slave.

The vampire watched in wide-eyed horror as Copernicus turned to him. "Your turn."

The young man bolted for the door and was caught by Shreve.

"What's the matter, kiss-ass? Not so keen now?" Copernicus demanded.

"I thought you were a vampire!"

"Are you saying I'm not?"

"You're mixed blood filth like the Hailemarris."

Copernicus backhanded the young man. "That's my sister you're talking about."

The vampire spat disrespectfully on the ground.

"I assume you don't care for my wolf side? Fine. The beast shall be your end."

Copernicus shifted into a huge wolf-beast. His jagged jaws clamped over the vamp's head, severing it from his neck. He spit the head out at the feet of the shifter before shifting back into his previous state.

Shreve dropped the body to the ground.

"Clean that up," Copernicus order the shifter.

"Yes, my lord."

Chapter Four

Wake up.

"No," Netriet moaned.

We're in his bed. You've been asleep the whole day.

Netriet opened her eyes. "What? All day?"

The evening is here. We need to go.

"I'm not leaving the Fair. I'm going to see Martia… Well, once I have something to wear."

Netriet sat up in the cozy darkness of Merick's tent. It was the best sleep she'd had in years. The noises of foot traffic and merrymaking sang a siren's song to her heart. Drums and lively flute music beckoned her to join the crowd. She stretched and ran her fingers through her silky, clean hair that had curled as it dried. The bundle at the base of the bed caught her attention. She unwrapped it and gasped as the clothes spilled into her hand.

"Wow," she whispered.

The amber velvet shirt fit perfectly. She ran her finger along the seam where the sleeve had been removed. Tears ran down her cheeks before she realized she was going to cry. Merick didn't borrow this from anyone, it was just for her. No one had done anything for her that made her feel special like this since her suitors in Christiana's court.

"I told him not to buy anything."

Well he didn't listen, did he? I don't know what you're gushing over. It's not even pretty. He's trying to manipulate you.

Netriet sighed as she pulled the pants on awkwardly. "I hate you."

I love you. The shadow whispered seductively.

She tidied the blankets on the cot as best she could and hurried out of the tent's flaps, instantly colliding into Merick's chest.

He grunted and braced his hands on her shoulders. She looked up into his face, and the warmth of his gaze ran down through her in a slow glide. How could he look at her that way? He saw her, *her,* not her scars, not her missing arm.

"Save me," she whispered, the words out before she even thought them.

His brow creased. "I will. If I can, I swear I will."

His hands moved over her shoulders and down her back, pulling her gently against him. For one moment, just one, Netriet breathed in and out easily, and his warmth continued to spread through her chest. The shadow pulled back in retreat from it. Then approaching footsteps broke them apart.

"Merick? You over here?" the voice called from the other side of the tent.

Merick pulled away, looking at her intently. "Go around to the front gate," he said quietly, before walking away.

Netriet listened to Merick greet whoever was on the other side, and the two of them headed off toward the merrymaking. She swung her leg over the sorry excuse of a wall and walked around the outside of the Fair toward the front gate.

Do you think he's so great now? The shadow mocked. *He doesn't want to be seen with you. He doesn't want people to think he cares about you.*

"He doesn't want questions. Neither do I."

Whatever. Let's get out of here. These people will never accept you.

"Coming here was your idea. I'm not leaving until I see Martia."

Fine. The shadow said tersely. *Go see Martia, and then we'll leave.*

"I don't think so. I'm in no hurry whatsoever."

A gruff ogre stood at the front gate halfheartedly on guard, clapping in time to the lively music. He turned his full attention on Netriet as she approached, crossed his impressive arms over his chest, and scowled down at her. His eyes roamed over her, assessing. Then the light of pity flickered behind the scowl.

"Who are you?" he demanded. "And what is your business here?"

Netriet smiled. "My name is Nettie. I have no business, so to speak. I'm a... uh...friend of Martia's."

The ogre's scowl dropped into a lopsided grin for a moment. "Martia is the most beautiful woman in Regia. She makes the best pie."

"Oh, uh sure." She didn't know how to answer.

The ogre frowned. "You've never had Martia's pie. Don't bother lying. I can tell."

"You're right." She desperately tried not to laugh. "I've never had Martia's pie, but if you say it's the best, I'm sure it is, and I hope I get the chance to try some. I *do* know her, though. That is the truth."

"We'll see. Martia!" the ogre bellowed over his shoulder.

Well, it was too late to change her mind now. Martia broke through the crowd and came toward the gate. Shock and then pleasure spread over her face when she spotted Netriet. Her smile was so genuine and maternal Netriet wanted to run into her arms like a child to its mother.

"There you are!" Martia exclaimed. "I thought you'd never come back!"

"Well, I—"

"You look better than the last time I saw you. Way too thin but certainly better dressed. What a beautiful shirt that is."

"Thank you."

"It almost looks like the work of…no that couldn't be. Well come in. Move out of the way, Koll, she's no danger to anyone."

"Just doing my job."

Martia patted him on the shoulder, making him blush. "And you do it so well, thank you." There was no sarcasm in her voice. She put her arm around Netriet's shoulders and moved her away from the crowd. "Are you feeling like joining the group? They can get a little rowdy, and everyone will be interested in you, so you'll be the center of attention."

Panic shot through Netriet all the way to her feet, making her want to run. The shadow was right. She should leave. She couldn't stand the idea of being looked at by that many people all at once.

"It's all right. Calm down. No one here will hurt you. No one will judge you… Why don't you come with me to my house, and I'll make you something to eat. We can have some quiet time to talk. What do you say?"

"Yes, thank you." Her voice came out in a rushed squeak.

Martia smiled and gestured for her to follow. Netriet gave one last glance at the crowd. Laughter, drinking, flirting, dancing, and eating. Her heart ached to join them. To be a part of them. Maybe she could be, but not yet.

She felt his eyes before she saw them. Through all the movement, her gaze snagged on his. Merick was watching her. He held her in silence with only his eyes. For one second, she felt that deep warmth again before the terror. The eyes are the windows of the soul, she thought. I don't want you to see what's inside of me.

With regret, Netriet turned her gaze away and followed Martia, her mind circling. What did he want? Why would he want anything from her? Maybe he was just bored. Maybe he just wanted to play with her, hurt her. He'd been both harsh and kind.

Forget him, my sweet. You don't need anyone. You have me. You'll always have me.

"Stop trying to cheer me up." Netriet kept her voice as low as she could. "You suck at it."

Netriet followed Martia, bemused. The ogre lady had an uncanny ability of making people feel they'd known her all their lives. Netriet frowned as she realized just being around Martia put her at ease, even though she didn't know her at all.

They walked to a row of small houses almost too cute to be real. Martia walked through the curved door of a magenta-colored cottage, its stone chimney climbing up the front in a charmingly uneven path next to a tiny second story window. Netriet stepped into the front room, delighted and jealous simultaneously. It was so warm and comfortable, as though the walls and knickknacks were somehow imbued with the happiness and contentment of their owners. It was a hodgepodge of odd, otherworldly things Netriet didn't recognize, not unlike Forest's house.

"Sit down and make yourself comfortable while I make us some hot tea." Martia walked into the adjacent kitchen and began clattering around. She was slightly too big for the space, but she maneuvered around it deftly. In a moment, she was back, pushing a warm cup into Netriet's hand and setting a large slice of bronze-colored bread on the little table in front of her. The sweet smell stirred her long empty stomach.

"I hope you're not offended by our house. The ban on Earth goods has recently been lifted, so I assure you, there's nothing illegal here."

Netriet smiled, the expression coming easier now. "You have a lovely home. Thank you for inviting me in. There are many who wouldn't."

"I'm so glad you're back. I was afraid I'd never see you again. Afraid something ill had happened to you."

The events of the night Netriet had first come to the Fair came back to her. Her gaze fixed on the patchwork throw draped over the back of Martia's chair.

"What's wrong, dear?"

Her eyes stung. "I lost the shawl you gave me...I can't tell you what it meant to me, your kindness. But I was attacked by two deserter wolves that night, and I lost it as I fled."

In a second, Martia had her arms around Netriet in a firm hug. "Oh, you poor thing! How horrible! How ever did you escape?"

"I stabbed one, then I got caught in Forest's damn alarm system, and she let me in. Protected me."

Martia let go of Netriet and sat back down, blushing a little. "She's a good one, our Hailemarris… Sorry for crushing you just then."

Netriet smiled and shook her head. The hug caused her hope of acceptance to sprout. Both Martia and Merick had physically touched her without acting as though she was something gross to be shunned.

"So what is Forest up to? I passed her land on my way here. Her new level of security is…impressive."

"You don't know?"

Netriet shook her head. "I've been very isolated for a long time."

Martia blew out a breath. "I guess so. It's the insurgents. The Aluka Circle, they call themselves. They've been causing so much trouble. But they are harder to track than shadows in the dark. As far as anyone knows, they want to re-establish the vampire throne. The strange thing is that their followers are not just vampires. People from every Regian race have joined, even a few werewolves. We had one come here a while back, a drifter. He gave us a song and dance about his past, made a few friends, then started trying to convert everyone he could. When no one did, and we knew what he was, that's when things got violent."

"What did you do?"

"Merick took him down. Delivered him to Forest. He's in jail, I think."

"Merick took him down? How?"

Martia laughed lightly. "Don't be fooled by his limp. That man is deadly. He's got the most skilled hands I've ever seen. I guess that's why he can juggle the way he does. Anything he touches can be a lethal weapon."

"Where did he learn?"

Martia narrowed her eyes at Netriet. "Merick is Tek's oldest and best friend, but he's very private. He'll have to tell you those kinds of things."

Netriet backpedaled quickly. She didn't want to seem overly interested in Merick. "Of course. So, the Aluka Circle—what do they do besides create converts?"

Martia shook her head sadly. "They're terrorists... Awful, unspeakable crimes." She shivered. "So many innocents have died... It's a 'join us or die' kind of thing. Forest will track them all down, have no fear."

"You seem very dedicated to her."

"All of us are, dear... Bless her, she's the reason I finally have a real house. All this change here at the Fair is her doing. We are now recognized as a legitimate town. And we have no fear of being punished for past offenses against us."

"She pardoned you all?" Incredulity crept into her voice. "I hope you'll forgive me, I too have a price on my head, but a blanket pardon seems a little...crooked."

To her surprise, Martia laughed. "Nothing about Forest is crooked. It would go against the very fabric of her personality. Now, she dabbled in some shady business with Tek before she became Hailemarris, it's true, but not abusing her power is everything to her now."

"So how?"

"She reviewed everyone's cases. Those of us that were outlaws, one by one. Some charges *were* trumped, those were cleared. She did arrest Simon, actually. He'll be out and about again soon enough. He didn't even mind that much. But it was the status she officially gave the Fair that protects all of us and those who come here. We are a City of Refuge. We screen those we let in to our community. If they pass, they are protected and can live in peace so long as they don't leave. Of course, anyone can leave at any time, but once outside the community, they will no longer have the Fair's special protection."

"I'm not sure I really understand."

"You will, if you remain."

"Am I to be 'screened'?"

"Of course. But since we are having a party tonight, it will have to wait until the morning."

She thought about it for a second, contemplating. The world she was sent away from, to Philippe, had been reconstructed. Christiana's court no longer existed. Her death sentence might no longer stand. She needed to figure out who she wanted to be now. Was she Netriet? Or was she Nettie? All at once, the nickname Philippe had given her felt disgusting. Why had she ever used it? So long as the shadow lived in her, she couldn't go home to Halussis, but she didn't need to hide her identity.

Stupid. These people will never be your real friends. Don't tell her who you are.

Netriet clenched her teeth together, refraining from answering the shadow.

"Netriet. My real name is Netriet, not Nettie."

Martia leaned back in her chair and smiled. "It's nice to meet you, Netriet."

She exhaled raggedly. The adrenaline required to say her own name began to slide away.

"Will you be our guest tonight? The bed in our spare room is wonderfully comfy."

The shadow writhed with panic.

"I'd love to."

****

Merick acted as he always did. He talked reservedly to his friends about nothing, politics, nothing, the upcoming bazaar, and more nothing, before the group began chanting his name over and over, to persuade him to juggle for them. He obliged, taking up the pile of daggers people laid at his feet. He moved into the center, everyone giving him room before he began tossing the blades into the air in basic columns, getting the feel of them in his hands, before shifting the pattern into a reverse cascade. The crowd clapped and loudly egged him on until he upped the danger and began backcrosses. All the while, his mind was on Nettie. His heart had held nervously still after he'd told her to go around the front, afraid she would climb over the wall and never come back. But she did, and Martia swept her away. He was pretty sure she wouldn't reject Martia's hospitality. He would let her be for a few days, maybe. The bazaar was coming. How could he watch over her with all that chaos? Would she run away?

Her lips dominated his mind. *Save me...Save me...*

He'd promised he would. How was he supposed to do that? Why did he want to? Why did she matter? She was broken. There was something wrong with her, something wrong inside her. She looked the way he felt. His mind drifted away from the here and now. His eyes drifted out of focus as the metal he juggled flashed the firelight over and over on his face.

Save me...Save me...

"Give it up, Merick," someone muttered as they walked by him, bringing him back to reality. Everyone was gone. The bonfire was languishing, the night growing cold. And he was still tossing blades in the air, his mind gone on autopilot, and the time had slipped away. He stopped and left the blades in a pile, feeling sheepish.

Merick walked to his tent, trying to recapture the contentment he'd had just the day before. He sat on his cot and put his head in his hands, still plagued by her lips. Damn, he wanted a taste. The desire bemused him. No one had made him want all these years since Geanna died, no one. He'd been through hell, spilled the blood of vengeance, and lived in the quiet sadness of his memories, but deep down he was still much of the same man he'd always been. He'd always taken action when he felt the urge or necessity.

Merick stood and walked back out into the night, unsure what action he planned to take but unable to deny there was definitely an urge.

****

Netriet couldn't sleep. She'd slept too long in Merick's bed to be sleepy now. Martia had been right about the comfort of the guest bed, but not even that coupled with her large dinner could make her tired. She stood, the hem of the borrowed nightgown falling down over her toes, and looked out the little window. Clouds smeared the moonlight. The wind sighed, and so did she. It seemed as though the shadow slept. Netriet had never had that feeling before. It was silent.

Netriet inhaled sharply. He was out there. She didn't hear anything, see anything—she just knew. He summoned her with nothing but the inherent knowledge of desire. She followed his silent call, down the stairs and out into the night without making a sound.

Her dark eye found him quickly, a short distance away, standing in the middle of a clutch of trees. She walked steadily to him, his gaze holding her again in the silence, only now it wasn't warm like before. It was hot, smoke, flame, and fever. She came within arm's reach and stopped. She opened her mouth then closed it again. Words were redundant. Everything about him spoke clearly. *I want.*

A low growl rumbled in his throat before he reached out, wrapped his arm around the back of her waist, and pulled her against him. She looked into his eyes for one second, and then he leaned down and took her mouth.

Merick's kiss wasn't hard, hurried, or clumsy. It was perfect. It was perfect until he ran his tongue across one of his fangs and she tasted his blood. If such things really were a battleground between men and women, in that one move, Merick won. Netriet hadn't tasted blood since the night she'd killed Philippe. Merick's blood tasted so good, full, and sweet, she wanted, *needed* more right now.

****

Oh, yes, hell yes! Merick thought as he kissed her. He hadn't expected her to just yield to him and then give back like she did. He savored, in no hurry for anything else at all. She pushed against him until she backed him into a tree. Now captive, she climbed him and sank her fangs hard into his neck. He was frozen in shock for a moment. *Whoa! That's not really what I had in mind but...all right.*

Her mouth pulled so hard, Merick became dizzy. Her mouth found his again, and she strained against him, desperate and begging to be touched.

What had he done to make her so crazy? She was trying to eat him alive. Her passion excited him, but it also rattled. Being pinned against a tree by a woman was hardly his style. He switched their positions and sank his teeth into her neck.

She gave a little cry and put her feet back on the ground, digging her fingers into the back of his hair. The first taste of her blood was sweet, but the aftertaste came quick, inky toxic, almost burnt. He wouldn't have swallowed, but it was too late. Then came the laugh. Faint like a whisper, someone or something laughed mockingly from *inside* him. From her blood. Shocked and scared, Merick pulled away from her. She came after him, clinging.

"Stop, Nettie...stop...slow down." He held her back.

She panted, and the dark in her strange eye moved and grew new tendrils. "What's wrong?" she asked.

"What's wrong? You tell me." He watched her eye move and change.

Abruptly, she shoved away from his hands, took a step to the side, and wrapped her arm around herself as though cold. She closed her eyes, her face pained. Inner turmoil played on her face before she snapped her gaze back on him, accusing and cold.

"Why did you come here tonight? Why did you kiss me like that if you didn't want me?"

Didn't want her? It had all been wonderful for one minute, now it was ruined beyond repair. What could he say? It was a mistake? Before she attacked him, she'd rocked him. Her sweetness sparked life into his atrophied heart. But now, he couldn't admit she scared him. He wouldn't. He needed to figure out what the hell was really going on with her, and until he did, he was too scared to touch her again. Whatever possessed her might possess him. Safer to cover it. When in doubt, act like a bastard.

He shrugged and crossed his arms. "You said I had no bite."

Her look of shock turned to embarrassment and then slowly shifted into cool rage. She took another step away from him. "Well, you sure showed me."

He watched her run back to Tek and Martia's house, hating himself.

CHAPTER FIVE

The crossed swords over Forest's head bore down. She pushed back with all her strength on the broadsword she held. The metal slid and scraped together. Her muscles shook. Sweat began to run down her back.

"Come on!"

With the last of everything she had, she cried out, a guttural yell, gritted her teeth, and pushed again against her attacker's blades. He was too strong. Dropping to the ground, she kicked out, sweeping his feet out from under him. She approached him, kicking his blades away. Forest pointed her sword at his neck, placing one foot on either side of him.

"It's not working," he said.

She thrust the sword into the ground next to his head. "Don't I know it."

He reached up, grabbed her hand, and pulled her down on him.

"Thanks for trying, again," Forest said, leaning down and kissing Syrus on the mouth.

"When you find the right sword, you won't have to go for cheap shots."

She nipped at his bottom lip. "I wouldn't be alive if I didn't fight dirty, love."

"So what's next?"

She laughed darkly. "I've gone through every new blade you've brought me. If I didn't know better, I'd say you were enjoying this."

"Of course I am! You've been working so much I don't get to see you as much as I want to. And playing around with swords in our garden brings back memories." He wiggled his eyebrows at her. "You know what memories."

She kissed him again, deeper. She knew what memories. "I'm so blessed to have you. Swordplay makes you hot."

He gave her ass a slap. "Swordplay *with you* makes me hot," he corrected.

She laughed and moved to get up. He grabbed her as he stood and whisked her into the house.

"It's my day off, not yours. I thought you had a meeting this morning?" she protested.

"It can wait. The whole world can wait."

****

Forest padded around in her robe for a while after Syrus *finally* left for work; he had all but rendered her totally useless for the rest of the day. She brewed coffee and contemplated her weapon problem. Losing her silver sword had felt like the death of an old friend, but now she was almost happy to be parted from it. It was tied to the pain of the past. She remembered the time and effort it took to make the blade, and its sole purpose: to kill Leith. Oh, she'd used it to inflict pain and death on more than a few vampires, but she never did hit her target. Syrus killed Leith. She wasn't really sorry his death hadn't been by her hand. She had rescued Syrus once; Syrus rescued her in return.

Forest put her hand on her stomach where Leith had stabbed her. She didn't think it meant anything, but sometimes she could still feel Syrus' electric healing power inside her body. It intensified when they made love. She wouldn't *ever* complain about that. It was fabulous.

She sipped her coffee and sighed. She needed to think about a new sword, but her mind wouldn't pull itself away from Syrus. After a few more minutes, she began to realize she wasn't just mooning over her love. He had the answer to her problem.

She dressed quickly and casually and used her personal portal to send herself to the Obsidian Mountain. Being the Sanguine's mate gave her the ability to go the mountain without invitation, but all the masters grumbled anyway whenever she showed up. It amused her. Menfolk and their little club secrets. She wasn't a vampire, and thus could never be a master, but she'd studied the Blood Kata, along with every other fighting style in existence. There was nothing done on the mountain that she didn't understand on some level.

She dropped into the mountain's portal chambers, kept by the ogre, Len. Huge and scary looking, Len smiled at her and jerked his head in a little bow.

"Nice to see you, Forest. The masters are doing forms right now."

"Gotcha. What do you think they'd do if I jumped into the middle and joined them?"

Len barked out a laugh. "Are you going to? I have to see that if you do."

"I was just kidding, but now, I think I have to."

She turned invisible and walked up the rock steps to the wide-open space where the masters, both accomplished and novice, moved in sync from their hands and feet down to their breathing. Syrus was leading them, his back to her. She knew there was no way she could sneak up on him. He felt her wherever she went. He continued leading the group without missing a beat until she slid up behind him and pinched his butt.

"Hey, sexy," she whispered in his ear. "Don't lose concentration."

Before he could turn on her, she darted away and maneuvered through the group, taking a spot right in the middle. Syrus smiled as she made herself visible again, mirroring his movements as everyone else did.

To their shame, it took ten seconds before anyone noticed her. Pandemonium ensued. The masters closest to her shouted in surprise and attacked without thinking or realizing who it was. She turned invisible again, ducking the punches flying at her, causing one master to hit another in the face. Shouts of confusion rose up from the masters around the edge of the group who hadn't seen Forest at all. She jabbed one in the chin with her elbow, sending him flailing backward. He roared and charged in her general direction. The entire group rushed around her like a mob. She picked her target, kicking him in the gut hard enough to send him falling into the master next to him, who tripped into the next... The entire hoard fell like bowling pins, leaving Forest standing in the center. She made herself visible again.

Syrus' commanding shout drew everyone's attention. "The lot of you are a complete disgrace! An unseen enemy came into your midst and routed you all in one move! You call yourselves masters? Every one of you will spend the rest of the morning in meditation. Now get out of my sight!"

"Yes, sir," they all mumbled, shooting her mutinous looks as they left the room.

Forest walked slowly up to Syrus. His face was stony, his arms crossed. When the sounds of shuffling feet and slamming doors died out, a small smirk pulled at the side of his mouth, then he snorted and laughed out loud. He grabbed Forest around the waist and kissed her hard on the mouth.

"That was hilarious, but don't do it again."

"Sorry, Len egged me on. I couldn't help myself." Forest looked around and spotted Len peeking around the corner, tears of mirth running down his rough cheeks. "Did you see that?"

"I sure did!" he chortled. "I appreciate your mate, Master Sanguine. She makes things interesting around here."

"Disruptive minx is what she is," Syrus grumbled.

Len chuckled more and went back to his post. Syrus took Forest to his apartments and shut the door behind them.

"I'm sure you have a good reason for coming here and ruining my class?"

"Sorry," she said lightly. "I came here for my new sword."

"What?"

"I had a brainstorm after you left this morning. A normal sword isn't going to be good enough for me against this new enemy. I need something special, and I need to make it myself. But I want your help."

Syrus raised his eyebrows in surprise. "Thank you. It means a great deal to me that you want my help."

The emotion in his voice sent her into his arms. She nestled against his chest. "I need you..." Her tone was soft and intimate. "I need you to protect me."

"You know I will."

"I know. What you don't know is, I'm going to let you."

Syrus grunted. "Huh. We'll see if you stick to that. I'm going to remind you what you said."

"Oh, I'm taking this threat seriously. I need a weapon stronger than my last. I thought if I could take some of the mountain... Would that be okay?"

Syrus frowned and ran one of his fingers over his lips thoughtfully. "That's quite an idea. I certainly don't have a problem with it. I'm sure Ithiel won't either. You're wanting the glass, aren't you?"

"Yes."

Syrus continued to frown for a moment before he nodded, and his eyes went bright. "No one has ever tried to weaponize it before. It's brilliant, Forest!"

"I was hoping I could take my time, find the right piece?"

"I'll keep everyone out of your way."

Forest wasn't sure what she was doing at first. She walked slowly around the walls, touching every place the obsidian glass broke through the black matte rock. The power of the mountain vibrated through its core like sound waves in a pitch impossible to hear. When she found it, she knew it. The jagged glass sliced her finger as she ran her hand over it. The small cut burned like she'd rubbed poison into it.

She closed her eyes and placed both her palms flat against the black glass. Power slid up over her skin to her forearms. She absorbed it. Concentrating, she attempted to will something of herself back into the rock, as though she might be able to commune with it in some way. Maybe it worked, maybe it didn't. She didn't know. She imagined the lines of the blade she would create from the hunk of glass. One thin vein snaked through the center, reminding her of a bolt of lightning.

The problem would be cutting it free. And she had no idea how she would fashion the shape of the blade once she got the glass loose from the surrounding rock. But she was determined to find a way, no matter what. And if the whole idea was impossible, Syrus would have told her as much.

Forest went to find a chisel. Her heart pounded with excitement and love for her new unshaped weapon.

After hours of cutting the glass from the rock, sweat ran down her forehead. She had to constantly remind herself to breathe, steady her hands, and work slowly. Syrus checked on her from time to time, but it wasn't until she had severed the glass from the mountain that she needed help. They wrapped the sharp block in a cloak so they didn't cut their hands and carried it together to Syrus' personal apartments in the mountain.

"Can I leave it here for now?"

"Of course. No one comes in here. It will be safe." Syrus pulled the fabric away from it. "It's a good choice, Forest. Powerful."

"I think maybe *it* chose me. I cut myself on it when I first touched it. The tiny slice still burns, and it still hasn't healed, even after all these hours."

Syrus looked at her cut, frowning. "You're going to have to be very, very careful. This sword may turn out to be more deadly than any I've ever seen."

"I know." Her voice was sober. "It scares me, but I can't change my mind. I already love it too much. It feels so right, but I worry about it being brittle. Will it shatter under stress or attack?"

Syrus grabbed a sword from the corner of the room and brought it down on the chunk of glass in a full, two-handed strike. The blade broke, leaving only a tiny nick on the glass. Syrus dropped the hilt of the now worthless sword on the ground and looked closely at the minute damage to the glass.

He came back to her, taking her cut hand in his, and shot a small red spark into the wound, healing it. "You should go home now, baby. Leave it with me. I have something I want to do to it."

She looked at him dubiously and then down at the glass and back to him. He gave her a look of challenge she understood. She sighed and nodded.

"Okay, okay. I trust you."

"I'll be home soon. The day is almost over."

She kissed him goodbye and went back to Len in the portal chamber, but she wasn't ready to go home yet. She opened her portal and went to see Shi.

As soon as her feet hit the ground in the wood, Shi materialized in front of her. Shi's transparent eyebrows rose as she moved through Forest's thoughts. "Interesting," Shi said slowly. "Can I contribute something to this weapon?"

"What do you mean?"

"What are you going to make the hilt from?"

"Umm…I hadn't thought that far yet," Forest confessed.

"Well, Syrus is adding something, I should be allowed to as well. I love you, too. I want to protect you."

Forest had only wanted to share her news. She hadn't thought to ask Shi to give her something other than her company and opinion. "What are you thinking?"

"Hold out your dominant hand."

Forest obeyed. Shi touched it as only a ghost can. At first Forest was confused, but as Shi moved her hand, she realized she was measuring.

"I'll be right back." Shi disappeared.

Forest paced a circle, listening to the sound of the waterfalls in the distance. In a moment, Shi was back.

"Here."

She placed the twisted hilt in Forest's hand. The wood handle fit her grip perfectly. She marveled at its beauty. It looked like a tree—the top resembled a canopy, the handle a trunk, and the base where she would insert the blade stretched down like roots, ready to grip the sword.

"Hold it up," Shi ordered, "as though the blade is already there and you are facing an enemy."

Forest held it up.

Shi placed both of her hands around Forest's hand and slowly let them sink through Forest's skin and bones holding the new hilt. Shi closed her eyes. A sharp jolt snapped deep in Forest's palm, and it felt as though Shi had fused her flesh to the wood.

Shi smiled and pulled back. "There. It will recognize you now. No one will be able to wield it against you. If it is ever stolen and used for evil, the hilt will break."

Forest was staggered. "Thank you."

Shi placed the whisper of a kiss on her cheek. "Go home and rest. The night comes. You should be with your love."

"So should you," Forest chided.

Shi shook her head, sighing. "He's always with me."

"*Talk* to him."

"I never should have told you about Ler."

"Forgive him, Shi."

Annoyance flared in Shi's eyes. "Mind your own business."

"Fine. Be miserable...I love you," Forest added more softly. "Thank you for the gift. It's amazing."

Shi nodded and disappeared. Forest sent herself home with her new prize.

She had two messages when she got home. One from Kindel, one from Redge. Both would have reports ready for her in the morning. She'd set Kindel to the task of finding everything ever written about Copernicus. And Redge would have intel from the field about the insurgents' movements.

Forest poured a glass of wine and thought about what she needed to do when she got back to work. No matter what she learned from the written history Kindel brought her, the best source for information she had was her father.

The next morning Forest found a pile of books and scrolls Kindel had dumped on her desk.

"Gah...I hate homework," she complained.

"Hey, I marked the relevant sections with bookmarks."

Forest smirked at Kindel. "Thank you. I guess you can keep your job, for now."

Ena came in with Redge on her heels. She took her seat in the corner, ready to record their meeting. "Before I forget, Baal is here," she said.

Forest looked pointedly at Redge. "Should we invite him into our meeting?"

"Up to you. I thought Rahaxeris was coming."

"So did I." Forest crossed her office and looked out the door into her waiting room. Baal stood with his back against the wall, looking bored.

"Where is Rahaxeris?"

He focused his ruby eyes on her. "Away, madam. Off world."

"Oh, he didn't tell me he was leaving."

Baal smiled slightly. "Can I help you instead?"

Forest mulled it over for a second. "Perhaps. Come in."

She shut the door behind Baal. Kindel and Redge nodded to him but made no other greeting. Neither liked Baal much.

"How may I be of service?" Baal asked Forest.

"What does the *Rune-dy* think about the insurgents?"

Baal's expression went blank. "Who?"

"Oh, come on." Kindel was incredulous.

Baal ignored him, keeping his eyes on Forest. She held his gaze, looking for insincerity. She got nothing, his eyes held her back, like running headlong into a wall. She didn't have time to screw around with him. It didn't seem out of the realm of possibilities that he didn't know anything. The *Rune-dy*, as a collective, didn't care about current events unless they were directly affected.

Forest crossed her arms. "All right. Tell me what you know about Copernicus."

Something strange flashed in Baal's eyes and then vanished. "I cannot tell you what I know. You don't have the clearance."

Both Kindel and Redge seemed to puff up with rage. Forest gave them warning glances.

"Thank you, Baal. Please inform my father when he returns that I wish to see him."

Baal smiled. "Of course."

She looked at the door. He turned and left. As soon as he was gone, Kindel began pacing the floor to burn off steam. Muttering things like, *arrogant bastard*, under his breath.

"I don't like him," Kindel said.

"*Really?* I couldn't tell," Forest retorted.

"Why does he skulk around here?" Kindel demanded.

"I need my connection to the *Rune-dy*. Get over it."

Redge smirked at Kindel. "You seem to hold yourself together when Rahaxeris comes around."

"That's because Rahaxeris scares me shitless. Baal just annoys the elf out of me," Kindel said.

Redge and Ena laughed at Kindel.

"All right, let's get this meeting going or we'll be here all day," Forest said sternly. "What have you learned, Redge?"

"I've been following reports of missing persons. Probably fifty this week alone. I'd say sixty percent of those have joined the Aluka Circle, based on the evidence around the disappearances. There's been some mangled bodies pop up here and there, nothing in the way of a hit from the circle. I'd say they joined and tried to leave or somehow displeased the leader... Trying to follow their movements is proving difficult. There was a hit since we talked last..."

Forest braced herself for the news. "How many died?"

"Six. An ogre family. Three young ones."

Forest slammed her fist on her desk, pushing out her rage, so she wouldn't cry.

"We need someone on the inside, a spy," Redge said.

"I agree. Do you have someone for the job, Redge?" Kindel asked.

Redge looked straight into Forest's eyes. "It should be me."

"No," she said quickly. "No way."

"Why not? Do you doubt I could do it?"

"Not at all. I know you could."

Redge regarded her silently for a minute. "You say no from your heart, not your head."

"So? You're my friend. And Syrus' *best* friend. I don't want you in that kind of danger."

"With all due respect for you and your office, I have fought in the front lines of three wars, earned more medals than anyone of my rank for a thousand years, led legions to death and victory, and babysat Syrus when he was a blood addict and a spoiled brat. I am greatly responsible for the kind of man he has become... And now I work for you. You chose me to head investigations and forensics. Have I not done my job nobly?"

Forest sighed and shook her head. "I meant no disrespect, Redge. Please forgive the insult... Among your many talents and skills, have you ever worked as a spy?"

"No," he admitted. "Maybe that's in my favor. I'll find what works, adapt, without thinking about protocol."

She mulled it over, hating that she had to. "I'll think about it."

CHAPTER SIX

Netriet stood in a large red tent in the center of a semicircle of the founding members of the Fair for her "screening." Tek, Martia, and Merick were there. Martia smiled and winked at her in encouragement. Netriet refused to look at Merick and tried to pretend he wasn't there, but being near him caused her heart to skitter and her cheeks to redden with embarrassment.

Questions about her past and illegal behavior were posed by Renee, the oldest-looking elf woman Netriet had ever seen. Netriet answered everything with as few words as possible. She told them briefly about her days as a courtier and the theft that had worked as the set up for her to be sent to Philippe. She left out details; some she couldn't remember after her transformation, and some because she couldn't stand to say them aloud.

"And how did you lose your arm?" Renee asked.

Netriet opened her mouth, but before she could say anything, Merick spoke up.

"We don't need to know that. It's too personal a question."

"I don't see it as that personal," the old woman rasped.

"Because you've never suffered a serious injury. If you had, you'd understand," he insisted.

"Fine, she can answer if she wants to."

All eyes focused more intently on her. Netriet chanced looking at Merick. His face was blank, but his eyes were anything but. She looked back at those sitting in front of her she didn't know.

"Thank you for the choice to answer. I assure you all, the circumstance around the loss of my arm is nothing that will come back to haunt me here.

All I will say is Philippe took it, and Philippe is dead. The rest doesn't matter."

When questions turned to her appearance, she clammed up. They asked about her scars and her eye.

What's wrong? The shadow asked, speaking for the first time since the previous day. *It's time to introduce me. Why won't you speak?*

Netriet held her mouth shut and shook her head, looking at the ground.

"I think we know enough," Merick said. "Let us vote."

Netriet chanced looking at him again, but he was looking away from her. She stared at his profile, confused. Why did he do that? Why was he protecting her now? She didn't understand. Had he been so awful to her because she'd come on too strong? Didn't most men like that? Oh, to hell with him and his inconsistencies.

They sent her out for their vote. She waited nervously by the front of the tent. What would she do if they didn't let her stay? She should have told them how she planned to make herself useful to the Fair even if she didn't yet know how she was going to do that. She would be alone again with no one except the shadow. How long would it take them to decide? If they cast her out, would she have to go right now? Would they consider her again if she came back after a bit of time?

Martia came out and clasped her in a tight hug. "Welcome to the Fair, Netriet! You're allowed to stay by a majority vote."

"So what now?"

"Well, I hope you will continue to stay with me and Tek until you find your feet."

The rest of the group filed out of the tent. A few nodded at her and walked on. Merick came out alongside Tek. He glanced at her uncomfortably for a second before heading off toward his tent. Last out was Renee. She looked at Netriet speculatively, seemingly interested in her velvet shirt.

"So you're the one who has Merick so tied up."

"I'm sorry?"

"Oh nothing, dear. Isn't that a beautiful shirt? Don't you think so, Martia?" Renee asked.

"Yes. When I first saw it, I thought it looked like your handiwork," Martia said. "Renee is one of our finest clothing designers," she explained to Netriet.

Netriet's stomach squirmed. "If you will excuse me, ladies, I have something…"

She walked away from them, keeping her eyes down as she passed people. They let her in. She could stay. She was so relieved and yet terrified at the same time. And all of it was eclipsed by her feelings surrounding Merick. She was to live here. How could she function around him? Would this insanity in her heart prove temporary? Could she learn to truly not care?

When she looked up, she was standing right outside his tent. Her feet brought her to him without the consent of her brain. She knew he was in there. Nothing but fabric kept her away from him. She could march right in and tell him how it was and how it would be, and that would be that. Manners dictated she should call out and ask permission to enter, but her anger over his kiss, as she thought about it again, pulled an override.

She pushed through the flap, and it all happened to her again. Her heart lost its rhythm as she fell into his eyes.

"I was wondering if you were coming in or just going to stand out there all day," he said.

All her anger and resolve drained, leaving her feeling tired and helpless.

"Why? Please tell me why you are like this, Merick? Is it just with me? Do you have a split personality like me? How can you treat me like I matter one moment and that I don't the next?"

"I don't know what you mean." His voice was harsh.

"Yes, you do."

Everything in his face and demeanor changed. He reached out and touched her cheek softly. "It's not on purpose." His voice went quiet and dark. "I'm sorry."

Her lip quivered. She couldn't stand against his tenderness, but she also couldn't trust it.

He shut his eyes tight as though he had a terrible pain in his head, and the hand on her face trembled slightly, the muscles of his arm constricting. He shook his head back and forth, stuck in some inner war. He opened his eyes again. It felt as though the ground had dropped from under her feet as he leaned toward her, both his hands now on her face.

"No blood this time," he whispered before taking her lips.

Again, she had no control. He touched her, and she gave it all up, as if control was too heavy a burden and she'd been carrying it around far too long. He held her immobile, trapped in his arms, but still she felt like she was falling. Falling fast, too fast—he made her vulnerable. Her heart longed for him, for what he could do, what he might do, but he'd proved unreliable. Her heart opened too fast and too fully to him, and it was too fragile. His harshness would rip it and wound it, maybe fatally.

Fool me twice, shame on me, she thought.

The memory of her embarrassment brought strength back into her body, and she pulled away, slapping him as hard as she could.

"What?!"

She stepped back from him, her handprint coloring his face.

"I get it, Merick. I'm too easy. Too desperate for acceptance and affection starved. Obviously, no other woman wants you, and I'm easy prey. Well, there might not be much to me, but what I still have I'll not give to you."

"I'm trying to help you."

"*Help,*" she scoffed. "You're trying to use me."

"I want you!" he yelled throwing his hands in the air. "I admit it. *Sorry!* But I want to help you, too. I don't know how, yet."

"I'll tell you how to help me. Stay away from me. Pretend nothing ever happened between us. I'll say *hello* and *goodbye* when our paths cross, and that's it. Don't lurk outside my window. Don't think about me."

"Don't think about you?" He laughed darkly. "I've hardly thought of anything but you since the first time I laid eyes on you."

"Shut up! You're a liar."

He crossed his arms. "Interesting accusation coming from the likes of you. I know the necessity of lies just as you do. Merick is not my real name just as Nettie was not yours. I've lied in my life, when I felt I needed to, either to protect myself or others...I ..." His face fell a little, and the depth of his eyes flattened. "It doesn't matter. You've made yourself clear. I'm sorry if my manners offended you. I won't bother you again." His tone was as cold as stone. He closed himself up to her.

There was nothing for her to do but turn and leave. She'd rejected him, and he'd rejected her. The gravity between them would be ignored. What might have been would become a faint memory of a moment of trial and error.

The sunlight fell brightly on her shoulders that now slumped as she walked away. Her one, treasured hand rubbed the soft fabric of the shirt he'd bought for her. Had she made a mistake? She'd acted out of fear. She acknowledged it. He would hurt her, she knew he would. Had his actions come from fear as well?

Netriet hurried back to Tek and Martia's house and let herself in when no one answered her knock. She went up to the guest room, laid down on the bed, and cried like a lovesick schoolgirl.

Don't cry, my sweet. Don't cry. It's for the best. He's not the man for us.

"Go back to hell."

I know what I'm talking about because I didn't come from any hell. I came from the world's heart. I feel everything. Feeling is all I know. And I know when it's true .Let me guide your heart. Trust me.

"Never."

****

Netriet carefully avoided Merick for two days. Then preparations for the annual bazaar consumed everyone in the Fair. She was flung headlong into the action, and she loved it. People were starting to remember her name. And since her skillset was still unknown, even to her, she became a gofer. She didn't mind. It was fun, and she didn't have to be in charge of anything. Merick, likewise, seemed to be avoiding her. She could forget about him…most of the time.

The night before the bazaar began, the Fair's usual evening party didn't happen. Three long rows of brightly colored tents sat empty and ready for the traveling merchants to set up their temporary shops in the morning. Everyone was exhausted.

Netriet sat at the table in Tek and Martia's house, enjoying a late dinner, when her happy bubble was popped.

Tek finished his dinner, pushed his plate away, and patted his stomach. "Well, I think I'll go to bed and leave you ladies to your evening chat fest, which I'm sure is about to ensue."

"I don't think I'll be able to sleep tonight," Netriet said vibrantly. "I'm too excited about tomorrow."

"Well, since you're so perky, would you mind taking this to Merick?" Martia asked, setting a covered plate of dinner leftovers in front of her. "He's on guard tonight. I always give him something warm when he has to keep watch all night. Poor thing, the cold makes his back ache."

"Oh…I…"

"What's wrong?" Martia asked.

Both of them were staring at her. She swallowed. She hadn't told them anything about her and Merick, and since she didn't want to, she quickly smiled. "Sorry. My mind had gone off somewhere else. Sure, I can take this to Merick."

She leaned against the front door, taking a deep breath of the cool night air. She would get it over with as quickly as possible. Hand him the plate, tell him Martia sent it, and come right back. Then the next time she had to see him, it would be easier.

He was leaning against the gate, his arms crossed, looking at the ground. His head came up when he heard her approaching, a scowl creasing his brow. She tried to keep her gait purposeful and meet his gaze defiantly, but his cold look made her so sad. She missed the warmth she used to feel in those dark eyes. The pull was still there, in the air between them, as strong as it ever had been.

"Martia sent this for you...she asked me to bring it."

"Thank you." He took the plate from her.

She hesitated a moment, unsure before turning to walk away. She made it a few steps.

"Netriet?" It was the first time she'd heard him say her real name.

"Yeah?"

He was smirking at her. "I've been thinking about you."

She opened her mouth then closed it again. Damn him. Her mind seemed to have stalled. No retort came to her, just the memory of the sensation of his mouth on hers. She squared her shoulders and kept walking. When Netriet got back to the house, both Tek and Martia had gone to their room. She climbed the stairs and sat down on the bed, suddenly and inexplicably tired. The shadow was moving in a way she had never felt before. She sighed deeply. It was like a massage, warm and comforting. Her eyes closed, and she lay back on the bed, hardly registering the lullaby the shadow sang quietly. Only a second before she fell asleep did she think to try to resist whatever the shadow was doing. Then it was too late. She dropped off as though drugged, unaware what the shadow was planning, unaware it was even possible.

****

Merick paced back and forth, his eyes and ears on guard, but his mind and heart had followed Netriet when she walked away. He cursed himself for the fool he was. The best thing he could do was leave her alone. He wasn't capable of saving her. He was pathetically broken himself. He pulled his memories from the depths of his heart and held them close. Geanna, his son Michael, his little girl Marah. He touched their faces. They were frozen, exactly the same as when they died. The dead didn't speak to him. No matter how much he wished, they never spoke.

"What should I do?" he whispered. "Can I love someone again?"

Movement in his peripheral vision startled him. He turned to see Netriet walking toward him. He was immediately alarmed, not that she was there, but by the way she moved. It was like the flow of water, steady and sensual. His alarm rose to another level as she came closer. Her eyes were closed. Sleepwalking.

He didn't move as she came within arm's reach and stopped. She opened her mouth and let it hang open.

"Merick...Merick..." His name came from her mouth even though she hadn't moved her lips. The voice was not hers.

He'd never seen anything like it, and it terrified him. "You know my name," he said gruffly, "but I don't know yours."

A terrible hissing laugh came out of Netriet's mouth. "Your bravado doesn't fool me. I can taste your fear in the air."

"Yeah, unless I'm mistaken, I've tasted you too, in Netriet's blood. And guess what, you taste rotten."

"I want you to leave Netriet alone. She's mine. You've hurt her enough already. She's been through too much for the careless likes of you."

"Oh, so you're worried about her heart?" he challenged. "I don't know who or what you are, but she doesn't want you. You've stolen away inside her, and you're the one who needs to leave. You're the one who's unwelcome."

Netriet's strange eye snapped open. The other remained shut. The black tendril moved and filled the entire iris until the amber color was completely swallowed in black. *It* was looking at him.

"Stay away, or I'll kill you."

"And if you can't?" he growled.

"Then I'll kill her."

Her eye shut, her mouth shut, and she turned and walked away. Merick watched, angry, terrified, and renewed in his resolve to save Netriet...somehow.

CHAPTER SEVEN

Baal swirled the clear liquid in the cylinder and held it up to his face. Tiny sparkles flared with the movement of the liquid and winked out as it became still. He took a deep breath and swirled it once more. The lights winked at him and died out just as quickly. His hand shook as he placed the cylinder back on the table and tried to school his rage and despair. The elixir was wrong, again.

His ruby eyes drifted over the stack of open books he'd taken from the *Rune-dy's* library. He'd found nothing in there to help him achieve his goal. He cursed himself. The fault must lie with him. He was too new in the *Rune-dy's* ways, still a novice scientist. He knew Rahaxeris could do it. He knew Menjel could do it. Maybe even Hezeron could manage what he attempted, but none of them would help. They would cast him out if they learned of it. Baal imagined shoving the pile of books to the floor and lighting them all on fire. The mental image brought him no satisfaction as he carefully shut each volume.

He wasn't giving up. He'd just go back to Maxcarion. He swore to himself as he remembered he owed the crusty old wizard. Not only would Maxcarion not help him again, but he'd probably fry him into a pile of ashes for coming back empty-handed.

He looked around his great room. The lamplight glinted off his treasures. His priceless collection of items imbued with power and magic. There were many things he could take to Maxcarion in exchange for his help, some he had purchased from the old man himself. But his heart ached at the thought of giving up even one. And the blasted wizard said he wanted an undamaged Talereneain artifact.

Baal paused. What had the old man said? The Fair. He could find valuable things at the Fair. He checked his clock. He'd worked through the night, and the morning was almost gone. He pocketed a small fortune of coins and grabbed a plain grey cloak on his way out of his cave. The sunlight burned his eyes. He yawned as he put up his hood, the night's fruitless work finally catching up with him. He went invisible before opening a portal to the wilds near the Fair, close to where Forest lived. There was no way he was going to drop his invisibility, unless he found something he wanted to buy.

****

The first light of day came through Netriet's window, waking her in a state of surprise. She hadn't remembered falling asleep. She hadn't even been tired. Merick had stirred her up before she came back to Tek and Martia's house, but then what? She couldn't remember. Now it was morning.

Netriet felt her cheeks grow hot, even though she was alone, as she remembered how Merick said he'd been thinking about her. She was sure she would run into him later, and she made a point to wash and comb her hair. She avoided mirrors as a rule, but she forced herself to look and try to work with what she had and not let it depress her. She still didn't have anything to wear except the clothes Merick had given her. She loved the amber shirt more than she would ever admit to him, but finding something new was on her list of things to look for today.

As the merchants began to arrive and go through registration, there was more noise and movement than she had yet to experience at the Fair. The shadow moved as though agitated or gleeful, she couldn't tell, and it remained quiet. No one seemed to need her help now, and she felt a little in the way. She kept her eyes open for Merick so he didn't catch her off guard.

As the makeshift shops were filled with eye-catching trinkets and wares, excited shoppers began filing through the Fair's front gate. Netriet moved to the sidelines and watched in amazement how the different cultures stood together in the crowd and conversed easily with one another. Forest had accomplished so much in such a short time. Netriet raised her head a little higher as she realized she had played a vital part in the creation of the new republic by killing Philippe.

As more and more people came in, a nasty thought came to her. She might run into someone who recognized her. Sure, she was telling the truth to her new friends about her identity, but this was her starting over place. She didn't want the past crowding her here. Or worse, a relative, realizing she was alive and dragging her back to Halussis. She shuddered at the thought and turned away from the attractive bazaar.

With the rows of tents as the main attraction, Netriet thought she'd be safe looking at the permanent shops of the Fair. A small store caught her eye; the front window was filled with beautiful clothes, fabrics, and jewelry.

A bell chimed as she opened the door and walked in.

"Welcome. Come in and look around." Renee, the old elf woman came toward her. "Oh, it's you, Netriet. I was wondering when you might come to my shop."

Netriet smiled stiffly. She should have realized this was Renee's store. Martia had told her about it. Not that she would have avoided it, per say, but the old woman had sharp, probing eyes. Netriet could tell she caught details others missed.

"Martia didn't lie, you have beautiful things," Netriet offered brightly.

The old woman smiled sideways. "Relax, girl. You're too high strung."

"I'm sorry. I didn't mean..."

Renee coughed out a gravelly laugh. "I can see I make you nervous. I'll take that as a compliment. But I'll leave you alone to shop...I know you're short on funds, so if you fall in love with something you can't afford, let me know. I might be persuaded to barter."

"How do you know I'm short on funds?" Netriet demanded.

"I know all kinds of things. Some I hear, and some I see and reason the answers. Don't be offended. No one's been telling me tales about you."

Before Netriet could think of a reply, Renee turned and shuffled away. She made herself a stern mental note to always watch what she said and did around Renee. The old woman was a detective without a case.

Netriet walked slowly through the shop, running her fingers gently along the fabrics. Memories rushed on her. Memories of Christiana's court. Times when her life was consumed in the details of dresses and jewelry. Sorrow clung to her memories. She'd been so ungrateful. Her life had been easy and filled with pleasure, only suffering mild irritations. But she'd also been narrow-minded. In some demented way, she was thankful for where she was now. Not thankful for what had happened to her, what she'd lost, or for the shadow, but thankful for a wider view of the world. Through trials, she'd learned she was a fighter. That was something to be proud of.

Her mind wandered in the soft sea of textures. A table laid with various blues caught her eye, and she moved to it. The shop bell chimed as someone else came into the store. Renee greeted the new shopper. Netriet thought about what Renee might offer her as barter for the sky-colored skirt she held. How long would it take her to work it off?

"Oh, that's lovely. Are you going to buy it?"

Netriet looked up into the face of the woman next to her and felt as though she'd been doused with cold water. Could her luck get any worse?

Syblee's eyes widened with shock. She looked almost the same as the last time Netriet had seen her, on the day Christiana had Netriet arrested. Syblee was always Christiana's favorite courtier. Netriet remembered Syblee's smirk as she was hauled away in chains.

"Oh, my! It can't be you! It's not you, Netriet. It's not you, is it?"

Netriet stood frozen, her heart breaking preemptively before Syblee could say anything else.

Syblee took a step back, an evil glint in her eyes. "It *is* you. My goodness, I thought you were dead. By the looks of you, I'm not totally sure you're not...ugh. I'd ask what happened to you, but I don't want the nightmares. The look of you alone is going to keep me awake at night."

"Leave me alone, Syblee."

"That's rude. Is that any way to talk to an old friend? Geez, you've lost your arm, and that eye! What the hell is that in your eye? Disgusting."

Everything inside Netriet closed up.

"Hey, bitch." Renee came up behind them. "I suggest you get out of here before I kick your pampered ass."

Syblee looked contemptuously down at the old woman and smiled. "I'm leaving. I wouldn't sully myself with anything Netriet might think is good." She grabbed a handful of fabric and pulled until it fell to the floor. "Oops."

Syblee laughed as she sashayed out of the shop. Netriet had turned to stone. She couldn't move. Renee patted her shoulder.

"Just breathe, girl," Renee ordered. "The past can have some sharp teeth."

The shadow rose to the surface like a tidal wave. *You're pathetic! Look at that old woman. She has pity in her eyes! Pity! We can't let this insult pass. Do something.*

"NO!" Netriet screamed at the shadow.

Renee jumped back, startled.

Then I will!

The darkness twisted and pulled, wrapping itself around her bones and muscles. It covered her heart, filled her eyes, and rose up her throat. It reached up from her depths and pulled Netriet down, down, down. Her reason was washed over with raw, unthinking emotion, crazed with lust for blood. Syblee's blood. She would have it. Right now.

Netriet became a passenger in her own body, unable to stop. Her vision tunneled on the shop door where Syblee had exited. She shoved Renee to the side and followed her target. Nothing mattered, not the people watching, not the consequences, nothing but Syblee's neck, breaking under her fingers, drinking her blood.

Syblee hadn't gotten far. The hair was first. She grabbed a handful and pulled so hard Syblee was jerked backward off her feet. The screaming was terrible. The shadow loved the sound of her terror. Netriet pinned her on the ground, holding her arms down with her knees. She slapped Syblee in the face so hard it felt as though her hand would detach at the wrist.

"You think you know me? You have no idea who you're dealing with. I'll show you."

Netriet grabbed Syblee's collarbone between her thumb and forefinger and pinched. The aberrant strength of the shadow pulsed into her hand. Syblee's bone snapped like a dry twig under the pressure of her fingers. Loud sobs punctuated her screams.

Ugh, shut her up!

Netriet sank her fangs into Syblee's throat. Her screams turned into a cough and a gurgle as blood filled her mouth. Netriet could end her life in a second, but that was too easy, too fast.

There will be more. More pain, more mutilation. She doesn't like your eye? Take one of hers.

Netriet raised up, licking the blood around her mouth and running her index finger under each of Syblee's eyes. Which one? The right one...yes.

An arm like a band of metal wrapped around Netriet's waist and lifted her off Syblee. Netriet kicked and thrashed to get back at Syblee, but she couldn't get loose from the arm that held her and whisked her away. Her vision still tunneled around Syblee. People rushed to her struggling form on the ground, and then Netriet couldn't see her anymore. She was in the dark of a tent.

The arms about her turned her around, still crushing her in place. "Netriet! Netriet, look at me! Look at me!"

The shadow stared into the dark eyes of Merick for a second before pulling back. He held her against his chest, his forehead touching hers, his eyes drilling into hers. Netriet writhed and bucked against him as the shadow retracted back down into a smaller and smaller place.

Netriet filled her body again, regaining back the control of her limbs. She cried and trembled, feeling as though she'd just been violently raped.

"There you are." His voice was relieved. "The darkness is leaving your eyes. I can see you."

"Did I kill her?"

"No. She'll live. It's not that bad really. Anyone might think it was just a fight that got out of hand. That's what we'll tell everyone."

Netriet was wrought with emotion. She was in control of her body, but her mind was still spinning.

"Let go of me. Syblee will live because you stopped me. I want her dead!"

Merick tightened his grip. "If you commit murder in broad daylight, in the town square, you will be tried and most likely executed. At the very least, you will be cast out with the murderer's mark on your forehead. Forever alone, just you and the thing inside you."

Netriet took a few deep breaths and nodded.

"Are you all the way back? If I let go, will I just have to chase you down and drag you back here?"

"I don't think so. No."

Merick let go and took a step back. As soon as she was free of his touch, the shadow moved forward again, in a testing little surge. Netriet charged back into Merick's arms.

"Hold me! The shadow hates you. She coils up away from you."

"Good to know," Merick said, holding on to her.

"That's never happened before. I didn't know the shadow could do that to me, at least not so completely. She didn't just take my body, she took my mind, too."

He held her gently, but with all his might. Gradually, the tremors in her stilled, and her breathing eased. He didn't know what to say. He didn't know what to do. She clung so desperately. He had to help her, but how?

"Merick?" she whispered, her head on his shoulder. Her whole body tensed again. "I have an idea."

"Oh?"

"Well, I…uh. There's something between us. An attraction."

"Yes," he said slowly, put on guard by her hesitation.

"And our attempts at affection have been… somewhat…"

"Is *disastrous* the word you're looking for?"

She let out a nervous giggle. "That one fits."

"What are you getting at, Netriet?"

She sighed and shook her head. "Never mind."

"Oh, come on. Just say it."

"Will you have sex with me?"

Merick felt as though she'd just clobbered him with the stupid stick, and he couldn't pry his tongue from the roof of his mouth. "Umm, why?' he finally asked. Why couldn't he just go all alpha on her and take what was offered? Oh no, he asked why.

"Well, I was thinking that since the shadow is inside me and she hates you, if you were inside me, maybe she'd go away altogether."

"I see. So, sex for medicinal purposes?"

"Essentially, yes."

"That's so hot."

Netriet snorted. "You can look at it as a favor for a friend. A kind of experiment."

"Experiment? You sure know the right words to throw around to get a guy's blood heated."

"Is that a yes?"

He hugged her a little tighter and placed a kiss on her forehead. "I need to tell you something."

"What?"

"Last night, you came to see me. Well, it wasn't really you. *You* were sleepwalking. It was *her*. She warned me to stay away from you."

"Wait, I was sleepwalking? And I came out to see you?"

"I just said that."

"Well, I'm having a hard time processing it, all right? What did she say?"

"She threatened to kill you, if I didn't leave you alone. And after what I just witnessed you go through, I think she could."

Netriet pulled away from him and began pacing back and forth. "She wouldn't do that. She's afraid of me dying. She's afraid if I die then so will she…I've tried to kill myself so many times, Merick. She never let me. It's an empty threat."

She came back to him and nuzzled his neck. "So what do you think about my idea?"

"Honestly, I'm terrified…"

"Of what?"

"You…of that thing inside you. I know I shouldn't touch you. It's risky, but…" He crushed her to him fully and let out a groan. "You'll never hear it said that Merick failed to help a friend in need. Particularly with favors or experiments."

He kissed her then, just a beginning.

"Netriet! Netriet, where are you!" Martia yelled, coming close to Merick's tent.

"There is, however, the matter of you attacking a patron of the bazaar to deal with now," he said regretfully.

She stretched up on her toes and pressed another kiss to his mouth. "I'll deal with this. Then I'll come back."

"I'll help you. It's not like fights haven't broken out at these things before."

"No. I'll answer for this on my own. I'll be back as soon as I can."

Martia opened the door of Merick's tent, blinding them with sunlight, and catching them in each other's arms. Her eyebrows shot clear up into her hairline.

"You idiots," she chided gently, coming forward, grabbing Netriet's hand and hauling her away from him. "You've created quite the stir out here, Netriet."

Martia shot Merick a dirty look over her shoulder as she pulled Netriet to face the music. He didn't follow, at least not where she could see him.

"What's happening?" Netriet asked.

"Well, the woman you assaulted has been cleaned up and is technically in the Fair's custody at the moment. She's just quieted down. Quite the hysterics… Care to explain yourself? I feel like the mother of a wild youth. First you're in a cat fight, then you disappear, and the next thing I know, I find you in the dark, making out with Merick."

Netriet blushed. "Sorry."

"As you should be," she said sternly. In another moment, Martia was snickering. "Go to Renee's shop. She's got your *friend* and has said she'll sort it out and make a judgment call. None of the elders argued. She has the authority. And the rest of us have our hands full out here with the bazaar."

Martia walked away, leaving Netriet standing next to Renee's shop. Her thoughts were still on Merick, then the shadow gave her a shake. Realization of what had just happened infected her like a fast fever. She'd attacked and tried to kill Syblee in the open, in front of people! Embarrassment and despair flooded her. Her past had brushed against her present, and the two made nasty bedfellows. For just a few short days, hope had come to her, but now she questioned if she should just leave and go back to her solitary existence.

Renee poked her head out of the shop's back door. "Well, get in here, girl. Let's get this over with."

The idea of seeing Syblee again terrified Netriet. Would she lose it again? She walked into the shop, her eyes down and shoulders hunched.

"Don't look so worried. She's not here anymore," Renee said.

"But Martia said..."

Renee waved her hand dismissively. "I sent her away with a stern warning to never come back here again, not that she would anyway. And I told her any accusations she brought against you would fall on deaf ears and likely land her in trouble. She wasn't in any way *keen* on seeing you again."

"Why would you do that?"

Renee locked the back door and shuffled to the front and locked it as well, turning her open sign to *closed*. She ushered Netriet into her back room, stuffed with her sewing stuff and half-made garments. Two little upholstered chairs were crammed into the side. "Sit down, Netriet. Let's have a little chat."

Netriet swallowed. Uh oh.

"Now, to answer your question. I protected you because, even though you are new, you are one of us. Each of us has things in our pasts we'd rather not come face to face with, as you did today. I'm not excusing what you did, but I understand it. However, there's something going on with you that I don't understand, and I intend to know what it is. Not because I'm a busy body, I am, but that's not the point. I saw something dangerous happen to you, overtake you. I can't stand by and let you endanger those I care about."

Netriet nodded, looking at her knees. "Of course. I understand. I would have tried to explain my *issue* at my screening but...I didn't want to and..."

"And Merick shielded you from answering," Renee said.

"I guess he did. I didn't ask him to do that."

"I'm not faulting him for protecting his lover."

Netriet's head shot up. "What? I'm not Merick's lover!" *Not yet, that is.*

Renee narrowed her eyes and crossed her arms. "I know about you two. Where do you think he got that shirt from? It's got blood all over it now. Shame."

Netriet looked down at the blood on her beautiful shirt. It was ruined.

"There, now. Don't cry," Renee tried to sooth her. "It's only a shirt."

"It's not only a shirt to me," Netriet sobbed. "It's all I have in the world. Merick gave it to me, because, because he's so kind."

"Take it off. I'll switch out the stained fabric with new. Good thing it's quilted. No one will be able to tell the difference."

Netriet struggled to remove the shirt and handed it over. She shivered, her arm covering her breasts, while she waited. She was amazed how quickly Renee worked.

"So, now that I have you at my mercy." Renee chuckled. "I'll whittle your secrets from you."

"You can try." Netriet smiled.

Renee eyed her sharply. "Are you dangerous?"

"Yes. I've proven that I am. But I was provoked. I've met many people here who would also be dangerous if provoked."

"Touché. That's true enough, but you're different."

"I'm not sure it's wise on my part to spill my guts to you. You admitted you're a busy body."

Renee laughed.

"Touché, again. All right, trust is earned, I'll grant you that. Shall we talk about Merick then? He's very handsome for someone so cranky, don't you think?"

Netriet bit her bottom lip and nodded sheepishly. She knew Renee was testing her, looking for chinks in her armor, but she was grateful for what the old woman was doing.

"How long have you known him?" Netriet asked.

"Long time. There, your shirt's done. Put it back on...I'm curious how it is for you, taking up with a man who used to have a destined life mate? Is that comforting, knowing he won't suddenly abandon you because he makes the famous first eye contact with *the one*... You look a little pale, Netriet. Don't tell me you didn't know?"

"I...I didn't." Too many feelings bombarded her. The shadow roused a little from her depths. "How could he not tell me?"

"I'm sorry. I thought for sure you'd know, being his woman and all."

"I am not his woman!"

"Oh, *please*. I've seen enough of how he looks at you."

"If I was his woman, I would have known he used to have a life mate." Netriet took a deep breath, but her heart began to tremble. "What happened to her?"

"Dead, along with his two children."

Sorrow didn't begin to cover what she felt. Merick's warm dark eyes came to her mind. She'd seen the old pain chiseled deep in his gaze, like a fossil. But never had she thought he'd have a loss so great in his past.

"How did they die?"

"No idea."

"What was her name?"

Renee hesitated. "Geanna...he should have told you. Your heart's tangled with his, despite your denials."

"Yes, he should have told me." Her sorrow alloyed with anger. She looked down at her knees again, shaking her head. "What I feel makes no sense, Renee. It's nonsensical and unfair, but I still feel it."

"What do you feel?"

Netriet met her gaze. "Jealousy."

****

Netriet left Renee's shop through the back door. The shadow moved faintly but remained quiet. She sighed and looked up at the sky. Too much day left for her taste. She'd told Merick she'd come back, but now…she just couldn't. Not yet.

I was right about him. Admit it.

"Not now!" Netriet warned the shadow through gritted teeth. "Don't talk to me again!"

Netriet jolted suddenly and looked around as though someone had called her. People moved in the square, talking, shopping. No one was looking at her. She moved away, making a beeline for Tek and Martia's house. She looked over her shoulder, certain she was being followed, but no one was there. She slammed the door behind her and shivered.

What is wrong with you?

"Aside from you?"

What are you running away from?

"I don't know…I should go find Merick."

No! We're done with him.

"Stop saying *we*! I am not you, and you're not me, and there is no *we*."

Are you really so sure of that?

Images of Merick holding who she imagined was Geanna conjured in her mind's eye. The jealousy was like a drink of poison. Jealous of a memory she could never compete with.

"He should have told me."

She went upstairs and laid down, exhausted, and just wanting the terrible day to be over.

****

Merick had forgotten how a woman could torture a man with waiting. Netriet had said she'd come back. How much trouble had she gotten into over that woman she attacked?

He paced in his tent, shifting back and forth between worry and fantasy. After a while, he couldn't stay put any longer and went to find her. He looked and looked, moving through the crowd of shoppers, but she was nowhere to be found. He combed the entire crowd, moving through the aisles of merchants three times, but still nothing. Frustrated, but needing to keep their discretion intact, he joined his friends and acted as though nothing was wrong.

When night fell, a huge party began in honor of the bazaar. Merick was forced to perform for the crowd. They clapped and egged him on, but he found no enjoyment in it. Just before the dawn, when almost everyone was quiet and asleep, he knocked softly on Tek's front door.

After a few minutes, he knocked again, and Tek answered, wearing his dressing robe and a murderous expression. His face softened a little at the sight of his best friend. "Do you know what time it is?" he demanded.

"I'm sorry. I just have to know—is Netriet here?"

"Yeah. She's asleep in her room. She wouldn't come out for dinner."

Relief sighed through him. "Thank you. I'll be on my way then."

Tek raised an eyebrow. "What gives?"

"Just making sure she's safe."

"Uh huh. Sure. You didn't tell me you were taking an interest. Better tread lightly around Martia. She's adopted the girl, and the smothering is only starting to commence."

"Noted. Thanks."

Tek shook his head and shut the door as Merick walked away.

Chapter Eight

Copernicus led the small group at a steady pace through the ruins of what had been a shifter colony just a day before. He surveyed the damage as he walked. Faint tendrils of smoke still emitted from the dying embers of homes that were now reduced to ashes. Copernicus was pleased how his followers had carried out his orders. Now that this area had been blighted by the Aluka Circle, the road was theirs. Regia was coming to understand and fall in line with his authority. No one would need to be warned to stay away from this place. The best route from his main hideout to the Wolf's Wood was now his.

The handpicked men behind him moved in silent tandem. All thirteen had been chosen for their ruthless, bloodthirsty battle skills. Today they would prove which of them could survive the ultimate test. No doubt some of them would die. Copernicus hoped not all of them. Even if just one came out alive, he'd be satisfied.

He took a deep breath as he crossed over the boundary into the Wood. He'd missed this place, gone for so long, but the beauty of the wood was something he could never forget. The particles of shadow sand floating in the air sparked in his lungs. His vampire blood dominated his other DNA for the moment, so he wouldn't react to the hallucinatory power of the sand.

He turned sharply around to his men. Only three of them were vampires, besides Shreve. He addressed the others. "This whole place is covered with shadow sand. Breathe shallow. Cover your mouths and noses with cloth. Follow closely, and don't be alarmed by the guardian."

A few of the group glanced around but made no other movements. Copernicus smiled.

"If you hear a female voice in your head, ignore her. You follow no orders but mine."

They moved forward a few paces. Right on cue, Copernicus heard Shi's voice in his head.

"I'm sorry to see you're still alive, Copernicus. You've changed. I see more inside you. More than Regia, I see the grafts of other worlds in you."

Are you going to try and stop me, Shi? He thought.

"For the moment, I'm going to watch and see if you can accomplish what you came here for today. Should be interesting. I'll enjoy the sport."

He smirked, raised his gaze to the canopy of branches overhead, and winked at her, even though he couldn't see her.

He moved in a straight line through the forest directly to the hidden home of Maxcarion. The magical illusion camouflaging the entrance was so obvious Copernicus found it almost laughable. Just his hand shifted into beast form and smashed through the curtain of rock.

He turned to his men. "Wait here."

He strode casually into the wizard's home. To his credit, the wizard looked totally at ease and not at all surprised to see him.

"I've been waiting for you, Coper. I knew you were coming for me when I heard the screams from the shifters yesterday." He shook his head disapprovingly. "I see you're still nothing but crazy with no style."

Copernicus sneered at the insult but let it pass. "Then why didn't you flee?"

"Look at me. I'm hardly the wizard who sent you off world so long ago. I'm weak and dying."

"Dying? What nonsense is this?" Copernicus came closer, taking in the details of Maxcarion's appearance. "You should have gone home a long time ago, Max."

Maxcarion shrugged. "Couldn't. I swore an oath. I had a duty to uphold the lie."

"Yes. And you've done your duty. You and the rest of the wizards who remain. Regia has no idea that your world still lives."

Maxcarion's eyebrows raised in surprise. "Why would you do that? Why would you speak it aloud now? I've been able to keep that knowledge hidden inside myself and away from that prying ghost all these years, and now you just gave it to her! Why? I know she heard you."

Copernicus smiled. "I have no loyalties to the wizards anymore."

"We took you in."

"I was tortured and experimented on! But I lived. And now, I am part wizard, too."

Maxcarion rose from his seat, rage puffing him up. "What are you doing? Why have you come back to Regia now?"

"The wizards plan for war. A complete takeover of many worlds, and Regia is on their list. Many will fall and die or become slaves. But not here! Here, with me on the throne, they shall fail."

"Rubbish! You're more insane than ever… *If* what you say is true, you think you alone can stand against an army of wizards? One on one, you might be able to win a fight with one, but this?"

"Shut up! I know what I'm doing! I will save Regia."

Maxcarion shook his head and sat back down. He straightened his cloak, combed his fingers through his beard, and picked up the book on the table next to him.

"What are you doing?" Copernicus demanded.

Maxcarion held up one finger as he thumbed to the last page. His eyes raced over the last paragraph. He smiled and closed the book, clasping it to his chest. "I wanted to know how it ended before I die."

Copernicus smirked. "And was it a satisfying conclusion?"

"No. Not at all." Maxcarion laughed. "The author left off with a cliffhanger."

"Damn authors. Too bad, old friend."

"Yeah, too bad."

"I'm sending in some of my best killers. A test for them. Please don't go too easy on them."

Maxcarion rubbed his thumb and forefinger together, and a spark of light snapped on. "I'm ready. Hopefully you won't have to come in after I've finished them all and do the wet work yourself."

"Hopefully... Goodbye, Maxcarion."

"Goodbye, Copernicus."

Copernicus turned and walked out to his waiting men. "All right, go in and kill the old man. Survivors will gain special favor and rank."

The men filed in, leaving Shreve and Copernicus to wait and listen. In three seconds, the sounds of terror and pain came pouring from the open rock. They smirked at each other when one of the men screamed like a little girl. The noise died off almost as quickly as it had started. Four of the twelve who had gone in came out, bloodied and shaking.

Copernicus clapped Shreve on the shoulder. "Take care of them, will you? I'll be right back."

"Father?"

"Stay here," he ordered as he walked away.

Once he was sure his men couldn't see him, Copernicus pulled power from his ogre blood and slapped the air with the flat of his hand. A portal opened for him. He walked out through the other end and stood before the Heart. The flames of the manifestation danced in a dull gray hue. He closed his eyes and took a deep breath. This was life, and he felt it through his whole body. Every part, every race, absorbed the power of the Heart in different ways.

"You want too much." Shi's angry voice intruded on him.

He opened his eyes and looked at her standing in front of him. Smiling, he reached out and ran his hand through her face. "I'd forgotten how beautiful you are, Shi."

"Well, you killed Maxcarion. Not sure if I'll miss him. He never liked me. Secretive."

"I know you've been all around inside me. Digging for dirt or whatever it is you do when you look in people's heads."

Shi crossed her transparent arms. "I don't see any hope for you. But then hope is not something I'm long on anyway."

He lifted a brow. "You're playing with me. I like it. You're not half bad at pretending you're not furious and terrified by me and my plans."

"I am confined to these woods. And thus very limited in my ability to raise the alarm. But I am determined to do what I can to stop you from hurting one I love."

"Who are you talking about?"

"Forest."

Copernicus licked his lips. "Ah… I wasn't aware you had an attachment to her. Little sister is full of surprises. The more I learn about her…well, she never ceases to amaze me. So, she's won the love of the renowned guardian. I'm jealous."

He turned and paced back and forth a few times. Then he took a step toward Shi and placed his rough, battle-worn palm gingerly against her ghostly cheek. She made no move to escape his touch; she just glared into his eyes.

"I love you, Shi. I love you so much."

"That's not love you feel, Copernicus."

He exhaled and nodded. "You're right, like always. I *long* to have a piece of you inside me. I tell my followers that I am everything Regia is, but that's not true. Not one drop of my blood is Dryad. I would swallow you whole, if I knew how."

"I want you to leave now."

"I'll be on my way soon enough. First, I want to know how you feel about the new information I've given you about the wizards."

"I don't trust what I see in your head. You're too divided, confused. You could be wrong."

"And if I'm not wrong? Will you stand with me to protect Regia?"

Shi floated back from him, scowling. "I'll never stand with a murderer like you."

He gave her his most charming smile. "I will find a way to make you submit to me, Shi. You can skulk around the Heart all you want." He turned and walked away from her. "The Heart, along with the rest of Regia, is mine."

****

Forest awoke to the sound of her phone vibrating. Syrus grunted as she rolled out from under his arm and sat up to read the message in the dark.

Forgive me, Forest. I can't sit still any longer. I'm going to join the insurgents to learn what I can and stop them if the chance arises. If you're honest, you understand. I appreciate the job you gave me and have, at times, enjoyed it and felt useful. But to tell you the truth, I have long felt a deep dissatisfaction with my life and its direction. My team is still there at your disposal. It's just me going rogue. I hope we meet again, even if I face criminal charges from you at that time.

Stay safe. Keep your guard up. Tell Syrus farewell for me.

Thank you again, for everything.

-Redge

Syrus sat up, wrapping his arm around her and placing a kiss on her bare shoulder. "What's going on?"

"Here, read this." She handed him the phone.

He sighed and handed it back when he'd finished. "He might not seem like it, but Redge is a complicated man."

Forest rubbed her hands over her face. "He's right. I understand. I didn't want to be the one who put him in that danger. He's done me a favor and put himself there." She chewed her bottom lip as Syrus rubbed her back. "I hope he can come through this."

"I'm sure he can."

"But with clean hands?"

"That will be tricky. He knows the risk he's taking. Redge never does anything without calculating first."

"He's become a good friend to me, Syrus."

"I know, baby. But no one is safe right now. I feel better knowing he's fighting for us from the inside."

Forest got up and walked to the window. She pushed the curtains aside. "There's not much left of the night. I can't sleep anymore now."

Syrus came up behind her and pulled her back against his chest. "What are you going to do today?"

"I have a few case files to go over, and I'll have to promote someone into Redge's place. New trials are coming next week. Kindel is really growing in his cross-examination abilities. I've got him watching Law and Order."

Syrus chuckled and shook his head. "You and your Earth stuff."

"Huh, don't act like you don't love it as much as I do."

"Oh, I love it, but not as much as you. Can you make some time to come to the mountain later? I want to show you something."

Forest was instantly excited. "It's my sword, isn't it? You've finished what you wanted to do with it?"

"Yes. I think it's about time you brought the hilt Shi gave you. We will have to test the sword's strength again, with the best blade we can find."

"I'll make the time! You can count on that."

****

Forest arrived at the Obsidian Mountain in the afternoon, her beautiful hilt clasped in her hot hands. She couldn't wait to see what Syrus had done. Couldn't wait to get her hands back on the hunk of glass. Syrus and Ithiel were waiting for her in his apartments, both of them looking intently at the black glass on the floor. Forest gasped when she saw it.

The vein through the middle that reminded Forest of a bolt of lightning was now illuminated electric red. Syrus' lightning. He'd infused his own power into the glass.

"Oh, my gosh, Syrus."

He smiled at her obvious pleasure. "Not bad, if I do say so myself. Now it will self-heal."

"Extraordinary." Her voice filled with awe.

But it was still just a rough lump of glass. It had to be cut into the shape of a blade.

"So what do we do now? How do we cut something that by nature can cut anything else?" she asked.

"Well, we've been puzzling over that," Ithiel said. "Just before you arrived, the answer became clear. It was so obvious it was embarrassing that we even had to wonder about it all."

They both smiled at her, waiting for her to catch on. She didn't.

"Who here in the mountain has a natural affinity for weapons?"

Forest felt like smacking her head with the flat of her hand. "Len! Of course! I should have thought of that from the moment I decided to make the sword. I need the help of an Ogre...duh."

"Shall I go ask him to join us?" Ithiel asked.

"No, wait," Forest said. "No disrespect to Len—I'm sure he's up to the task, but this sword is so personal to me, I'd like to call on a close friend for this. I'll be right back. Merhl is at the Onyx Castle. I'll just pop over there and bring him back."

Forest used her portal to jet to the Onyx Castle. She landed in the vacant throne room. The thrones had been removed since the last time she'd been there. She smiled. Zeren had wanted to do that for a while. She left the room and headed out down the hall. She expected to have to track Merhl down, but he came around the corner at the end of the hall and stopped dead when he saw her. She smiled and waved, but her jovial greeting was not returned. Merhl rushed to her, his face pale.

"What's wrong?" she demanded.

"You shouldn't be here!" he whispered urgently.

Her mind raced to worst-case scenario.

"Zeren is writing to you right this minute to warn you to stay away from here. It's not safe for you here. Too many people come through here every day. We just caught one of the insurgents before they could kill an entire room of people. I locked him up, but he started raving about you. They're after you, Forest. You're a target!"

Forest placed her hands bracingly on his massive shoulders. "I know they're after me, Merhl. They've been threatening me for a while now."

His eyes widened with shock and horror. His concern warmed her heart.

"If only I had known before now. I would have begun a plan to do what I can to protect you, my lady."

"Well, that's why I'm here, actually. I came to see if you could come with me to the Obsidian Mountain. I need your help with a new sword."

"Of course. Just get out of here. I'll tell Zeren I'm leaving, and I'll meet you there in a few minutes."

"Thanks, Merhl."

Merhl was as good as his word and arrived at the Obsidian Mountain minutes after Forest. Forest, Syrus, and Ithiel all watched in silence as Merhl surveyed the black glass. He stooped over it and ran his palms along the jagged surface. Forest winced, certain that his hands would be sliced to ribbons, but he suffered not one cut.

"Come here, Forest," Merhl instructed. "I am going to close my eyes. You will direct my hands, and together, we shall accomplish it."

Forest got down on her knees beside the glass with Merhl behind her. He reached his long arms around her. She placed her hands on top of his and couldn't help the rush of pity she felt. His hands, so gifted, so full of magic, were gnarled and elongated, twisted with pain. The power throbbed up from his hands into her palms. She took a deep breath and imagined the shape she wanted the sword to take.

"Visualize the blade as you direct my hands. Imagine we are sculpting it, as if the glass were sand."

She took another deep breath and placed just a tiny amount of pressure onto his hands. The rough glass beneath his palms compressed and smoothed out like wax beginning to melt. Forest moved Merhl's hands very slowly, erring on the side of caution, knowing even the slightest wrong move could ruin the entire blade. Nervous sweat began to drip down her head even though she exerted hardly any effort.

Her new sword emerged from the shapeless lump of glass, perfectly balanced and sharper than any diamond-cut razor. All four of them gazed on it reverently in silence. Forest handed Merhl the hilt, and he fit it into place in seconds. Warm yellow light glowed out between his fingers. The light ran down through the interior of the hilt, into the glass. It slid like thick liquid, illuminating around the vein of lightning and then down to the tip of the blade where it pooled, sparked, and then died out.

Merhl smiled, swung the sword in a large arc, and then handed it to Forest.

Her hand shook slightly as she took it. The hilt was still warm. It was larger than her last sword, broader, and longer, but it was the perfect weight.

"I've never seen a more beautiful weapon," Merhl said. "Thank you for including me in its creation."

"Thank you, for helping me."

He bowed to her and nodded to Syrus and Ithiel in turn. "I must get back now. If you need me again, please send word or someone else to fetch me." He gave her a severe stare. "Don't come back to the Onyx Castle again."

"What's this?" Syrus asked.

"Nothing," Forest said quickly.

Syrus narrowed his eyes at her then looked back at Merhl.

"We caught one of the insurgents today at the castle. Once we restrained him, he began raving about Forest and some plot to take her out. I don't feel the castle is a secure location for her right now, as so many people come through there. That's why I need to hurry back. We have to formulate new security measures, not just to protect Forest, but the public as well."

"Let us know if there is anything the masters can do to help," Ithiel said.

"Thank you, Master Ithiel. I will." Merhl gave them all another little bow. "Please excuse me." Then he left.

Syrus rounded on Forest.

"Don't look at me like that, Syrus. I didn't know about it until I got there to get Merhl. I don't put myself in danger on purpose."

He raised one eyebrow and sighed, shaking his head, but he swallowed whatever reprimand he had bubbling up his throat and turned to Ithiel. "I think it's time we formulated our own plan to fight Copernicus."

Panic surged through Forest. Along with all kinds of irrational arguments she wanted to throw at Syrus. She wanted him out of it. She wanted Syrus safe and tucked away in the mountain. But instead of flying into female hysterics and humiliating herself, she clamped her mouth shut. What she wanted was irrelevant. If the situation were reversed and Syrus was the target, not even the fire of hell would stop her from doing everything she could to protect him.

Ithiel nodded sagely. "It's only a matter of time, and we don't know how much, before he comes here and tries to take the mountain. You know he'll want it. I think we might be overconfident in our abilities to protect ourselves. The mountain has been under siege before, but never by something like this, something we don't really understand."

"We need to gather everyone, even the novices. Everyone must be in agreement."

Ithiel and Syrus looked at Forest pointedly. As much as this was her business, it really wasn't. She had no right to sit in or have input in a meeting of the masters. And as much as she wanted to give them a piece of her mind about what they should or shouldn't do in this matter, again she kept her mouth shut. She carefully set her sword on the floor.

Syrus understood everything in her eyes. "Give us a minute, Ithiel. I'll be right down."

Ithiel bowed out of the room graciously.

Neither one of them moved toward the other. Their bond of heat, light, and spirit pulled together, invisible in the air between them. Their eyes bound. Their hands bound, and their souls bound.

"I love you." Her love for him pulled so tight it almost choked the air from her lungs.

"And I love you."

"Whatever you decided to do, please—"

"Don't ask me to promise you things I cannot, Forest."

She pleaded to him from her heart. He rubbed the heel of his hand over his chest as he received her message. He shook his head gravely.

"In my heart, there is only you and me, the world be damned... But in reality, the world is more than you and me. And both of us are leaders. We have to think of those we lead, those we protect. We must act worthy of our positions."

"We could run away. Just you and me. Remove ourselves from the equation."

He smiled. "You don't mean that."

She sighed and shook her head. "Only in my dreams."

"Nothing has changed. You and I live separate lives. We work separate, if not similar work. But our souls are bound together, eternally. Don't think, for one second, I will ever do anything without that as the center of every thought and action I make." He reached out for her then and enveloped her in his arms.

"Decide slowly, Syrus. Without you, I am nothing."

He placed her hand over his heart. "Without you, I don't exist."

They kissed slowly.

"Go now, Forest. Take that badass blade with you and get it a scabbard."

Forest picked the sword up and brandished it at him. "I'll need to practice with it."

He gave her a hot look. "I guess I can suffer through sparring with you."

CHAPTER NINE

Netriet moved along the vendors, her vision sliding over the goods and trinkets for sale, not really seeing anything. She was doing all she could to lock down thoughts of yesterday. It frightened her more that the shadow had not mentioned it all morning. It remained silent, leaving her wondering why.

Music struck up behind her. She half turned but stopped dead when she heard people clapping and chanting Merick's name over and over. She was not going to look at him, not going to watch him perform. She hadn't yet controlled her unreasonable jealousy and anger over his secrecy. She kept her eyes down and moved over to the next row of vendors, where her vision would be obstructed by temporary tents if she gave into temptation and tried to look at him.

The sensation of being watched slithered up her spine again as it had the day before. Her muscles tensed as if she expected a strong wind to push her from behind, shivers sliding out onto her skin. She turned, her gaze captured and held. A jolt went through her stomach.

Oh, yes please. The shadow purred.

She could no longer hear the music in the square. All that was in her ears was the laborious pounding of her heart as though her pulse had slowed, or the passing of time had compressed in the moment.

Never had she seen anyone who seemed so wrong. Not beautiful like Merick, or Syrus, yet he was sexually compelling, devastatingly so. A small smile curved one side of his mouth, that some might say was built for sin, but Netriet saw deeper. He wasn't built *for* sin, he was *made* of it. A personification of danger, allure, power, and quite possibly…evil.

She held still as he moved toward her, never for a second breaking his ruby gaze from hers. His long elf fingers reached out and took her hand, bringing it smoothly to his lips. Sparks and snaps erupted on her skin where his lips touched. Hot and cold moved up through her hand to her wrist, all the way up her arm, till the sensation entered her chest and burrowed into her heart. Another jolt shot through her stomach.

"At last I've found you," he said. "My love, my destiny."

"What do you mean?"

"Did you not feel the shiver and pull of the bond? I did. The second our eyes met, I felt it. You're my mate."

Netriet's head swam as though she were sick or hallucinating. "What's your name?"

He kissed her hand once again and smiled. "Baal. And yours?"

"Netriet," she half squeaked.

"Come with me," he whispered. The resonance of his voice was the fabric of seduction, and he wrapped it around her like silk.

He took her hand and led her away. It was like being caught in the tide. He pulled her from everything. She floated away from the Fair without a backward glance or thought. Powerless against this devastating gravity. A portal opened and swallowed them both. She hardly noticed. She held Baal's hand. The hot and cold sensation continued to slide seemingly from his palm into hers. Her mind rolled. Mate. She had a destined life mate. And he was an *elf*.

She watched his profile as they stepped out of the portal. The sunlight glided along the shafts of his ebony hair, teasing out glimmers of blue. He moved with the fluid grace of a predator shadow. Was this how it was for everyone when they found their mates? Like an instant addiction? The flow of sensation from his flesh into hers took ahold of her DNA. It was like a strange, cold light, incased in smoke, traveling though her, sparking and snagging on her joints. It caressed and entered her cells and finally pooled in her lower abdomen, where it moved, arousing her in a totally off and wrong way.

He continued to pull her along, and she followed without looking where they were going. She only looked at him. He was the tide. She went where he led.

She had the feeling they were going underground. The sound of rock sliding against rock, and the sun was gone. All was dark for a moment. Then his eyes were on hers, and his lips were on hers. She drowned. He was a dark current, an abyss of night, and he pulled her under. The shadow filled her extremities, straining to touch him. The caress of the shadow promised an unknown pleasure. Baal's lips promised an unknown pleasure, and Netriet was caught between the two.

Give in, Netriet. Just give in.

Baal pressed, the shadow pressed, and she could hardly breathe. Her mind stretched up, like the hand of the drowning, reaching for any hope of rescue. *Merick.*

There is no Merick, my sweet. There is only Baal. Baal is the world now.

The last of her oxygen expelled from her lungs. Baal was in her mouth, the shadow was in her mouth. There was nowhere to go. No salvation. He was the tide.

****

Netriet was sure someone had driven a spike into her head. Unfamiliar sounds and smells surrounded her. She listened, unwilling to chance opening her eyes yet. She rolled to her side; the softness of fur caressed her bare skin. For one terrible second, she feared she was back in Philippe's bed, covered by a werewolf pelt. But nothing around her smelled of wolf.

She groaned as another spike drove into her head alongside the first. What had happened? Obviously, she'd been sleeping. She didn't remember falling asleep. The touch of the fur along her body made her more than aware she was naked. When did she remove her clothes? She couldn't remember. She was crashing inside herself. Her body stung and craved. It was like hunger, a very singular hunger that had nothing to do with food or blood. She needed the heat and the cold back.

She gasped, her eyes shooting open as a hand ran up her hip and onto her back. The light was dim and softly blue, but it still stabbed needles of pain into her eyes. She looked into deep red eyes, and flashes of memory came back to her like the fragmented remnants of a dream. Her cheeks burned at what she remembered. Pain, pleasure, and depravity. What had he done to her?

She was in bed with a stranger. She'd never done such a thing before. Humiliation swamped her. She had to get away from him. She had to get back to…where? He was her mate. She knew nothing but his name, but he was hers. And whatever had happened between them was all right. It was all right, she soothed herself. It was all right. The deed was done…now she just needed to get to know him. He was her future.

Baal, her life mate. She was mated to a *Rune-dy*. She reached up, a little self-consciously, and touched his face. He half flinched, then he smiled. She studied him. *He's hideous, and he's gorgeous*. His features were sharp, angular, and unique. He was striking and sexual, but yet so odd. Somehow beautiful and exotic in his ugliness.

"So, my love, how do you feel today?" he asked.

She shivered just as she had the first time she'd heard his voice. "Used," she admitted honestly.

He laughed quietly. "I hope so. I admit I feel that way myself. You've got some *interesting* appetites."

Netriet grimaced and groaned. "I'm sorry. I really don't remember much of what we did."

He looked concerned. "Do you have memory problems?"

"Uh…sometimes," She had to tell him everything. She wished they had talked before diving into bed. Perhaps the pull of the bond was too strong for him to wait.

"We have much to learn about each other," he said. "Perhaps you'd care to get dressed before we share our histories? I don't want you to get cold."

She nodded. He rolled away from her. She watched him, mesmerized by the way he moved as he pulled on simple clothes. His movements made no sound at all. Netriet looked around for her clothes. It was the first she was seeing of her surroundings. It had been so dark before; all she had seen were his eyes.

The place looked like a cave. Everything was grey stone, even the bed she lay on was a solid stone slab draped with furs. She ran her hand over the fur, certain she had no idea what kind of creature it came from. She only knew it was not werewolf. Strange light came from the far corners of the huge, dome-like room. A table set with books and scary looking instruments dominated one side, surrounded by shelves of trinkets, glass, and stone jars. Odd-colored light emanated from some of the jars. A faint vibration, like music, came from one.

Not that she knew much about the *Rune-dy,* but she certainly had never heard about one having a life mate. It seemed wrong. She shook herself, realizing it was just her ignorance. She knew most of the rumors about them were just that, rumors, meant to create fear. At least she sincerely hoped so. Still, what did it say about her? That destiny would pair her with him?

Her mind twisted back to Merick, and she wanted to cry.

Stop that right this second! You must never think about him again. It's unfaithful.

Netriet looked back at Baal, ashamed of her errant thoughts. She was confused. Was there something wrong with their bond? It seemed weak to her, fragmented. The fault must be with her. She was broken, possessed with an evil entity. Surely that was the reason she questioned, the reason her heart hesitated. He gazed at her steadily, his look teasing out a shiver on her skin.

She couldn't deny he excited her. He was dangerous. Warning emanated all around him. He wasn't warm or comfortable, all sharp edges. Beautiful sharp edges.

Netriet spotted her clothes on the floor a few paces away. "Would you hand me my clothes, please?"

He smiled and crossed his arms over his chest. "No."

She took a deep breath, braced herself, and stood. The fur fell away as her feet touched the cold stone floor. Okay, intimacy here we come. Nothing to be self-conscious about, she thought. The thought almost settled before she heard his sharp intake of breath. Looking at the ground, she forced herself to look up at him, watching at her. She feared she'd see pity in his eyes, but what was there was far worse. Distaste.

His eyes roamed slowly over her naked frame, stopping on each black scar that marked her ivory skin. Tears spilled slowly from her eyes. Not even her life mate found her beautiful. She quickly made to cover herself, but he was faster.

Baal got up and grabbed her clothes from her hand. "You misunderstand me, Netriet. You don't need to hide yourself from me."

"You think I'm ugly."

"In a way, yes. But it's probably not what you think. Come here." He took her by the hand and led her across the room. The flat gray of the stone on the wall shimmered when he touched it and became as reflective as a mirror. "Look closely at yourself," he commanded. "What do you think is ugly?"

"My scars, my eye."

"Wrong." He ran his index finger along the length of her longest scar, on her shoulder. "This is your beauty, your power. You have an elemental strength inside you, if only you wouldn't fight it. It's here." He pointed to where her arm used to be connected to the rest of her. "This is what's ugly. I hate imbalance, Netriet."

She looked down. "I'm sorry there's nothing I can do to fix that."

He tilted her chin up with one long finger, forcing her to look at her reflection again. "I can."

She looked at him in the mirror. He was serious.

"How?"

"I am a *Rune-dy*. I have access to technology and medicines from many worlds. I can give you a new arm, superior to the one you lost. Would you like that? Would you let me?"

"Will it hurt?"

"I'm sure it will, yes. Terribly."

"Can I think about it?"

He smiled and took a step back from her. "Of course."

She turned from her reflection. "Can I have my clothes back?"

He handed them back to her and watched her struggle to get into them. Again, he looked at her with distaste and shook his head. He ran his finger along the seam of her shirt where Renee had altered it for her. "I hope you won't think too long about a new arm… This is embarrassing."

Netriet flinched. Was he cruel, or just too honest?

"Come, sit with me." He took her hand. "Let's begin to get to know one another."

****

Gone. Netriet was gone. He'd lost her. He'd come so close, only to have her slip through his fingers. The pain staggered Merick. He couldn't breathe. Was she hurt? Was she cold? Was she alive? Had she run away from him?

All of his investigating since her disappearance left him with one eyewitness who had seen her leave with someone, through a portal, and Renee recounting her last conversation with Netriet. He'd almost throttled the old woman when she told him about spilling to Netriet about Geanna and how Netriet had taken the news. He told Martia what he'd found out and then sought solitude.

Sitting alone on his cot with his head in his hands, the weight of failure slowly cranked a vise on his heart. The screams of his children and mate as they died filled his head. The smell of their flesh as it burned seemed to choke him. He felt the phantoms of the blades that stopped him from saving them. Then they faded away, and all that was in his head was Netriet. He couldn't change the damnable past, but he didn't have to sit here and do nothing. He'd sworn an oath to her.

Save me…Save me…

Strength flowed up his spine as he stood. He'd find her. No matter what.

CHAPTER TEN

"What's back here?"

"Don't go in there!" Baal shouted, making Netriet jump back from the door.

"Why?"

"You're not ready for what's in there, sweetheart." He softened his tone. "You're too innocent, still. A little while longer with me, and no one will think of you as innocent. But for the time being, stay out of there."

Netriet sighed, trying not to be angry, and went back to sitting on the stone bed and looking at the strange book he'd given her to read. As far as she could tell, they'd been cloistered together in Baal's odd abode for two straight days. It wasn't what she would call a honeymoon period. Since she'd arrived here with him and their initial consummation, he had hardly touched her again. She knew a great deal about him now and a little about what he did as a *Rune-dy*. In turn, she had spilled her guts to him, everything she could remember. He listened attentively but grew agitated at the things she couldn't remember. When she had talked herself out, he went to his desk and began pouring over books and making notes furiously.

She looked over at him. He was screwing around with some liquid mixture in vials. She was bored.

He looked up at her and smiled. "Sorry. I'm about finished with this. Then I'll have to take my results in to work."

"Can I come with you?" she asked hopefully.

He laughed. "No, you can't. Trust me, you don't want to. Menjel would put you on his table and dissect you, literally. And since Rahaxeris is gone, he's doing all kinds of things, off the books, so to speak."

Netriet shuddered.

"Yes. That is the proper response, my love."

"Rahaxeris is the high priest, right?"

"That's right."

"And he's Forest's father?" she asked.

"Right again."

"Is he bad like Menjel?"

"Bad?" Baal arched one sharp eyebrow. He put everything down, his movements deliberate. He moved toward her as if she were his prey.

She stood, her heart instantly beating hard and fast.

"Is *he* bad?" His voice had turned to silk as he lowered his face an inch from hers. "So naïve," he whispered. "Everything is about power. Rahaxeris has the most, so he is our leader."

He put his hands on her, and her skin lit up under his long, elegant, terrible fingers. He rubbed along the length of the scar on her neck with his index finger, over and over, like a cool breath. Goosebumps rose on her skin as her nerve endings became hypersensitive. Netriet gasped at the sensation. That one touch from his finger was more sexual than anything she'd yet experienced. What was he doing to her? The shadow purred and throbbed under his touch.

"We are all bad, Netriet. If it were about that, I would be the leader, because of all the *Rune-dy...* "

He kissed her mouth, and her knees gave.

"...none is as *bad* as me, baby."

Her whole body pulsed. The shadow rushing through her raged for more of him. She lay back on the stone bed. He looked down at her, his face going blank.

"Later..." He turned and walked back to his desk. "I have to go in to work now. Stay here. Don't leave."

Embarrassed, she scrambled to her feet. "Why do I have to stay here? I want to go see my friends and tell them I'm okay and I've found my life mate."

He sighed. "I'm trying to protect you. Why don't you write your friends a letter instead?"

"I guess I could, but I don't want to stay here by myself. I'll be lonely and bored."

He came back and pecked her lightly on the mouth. "Stay here. Once you leave the cave, you'll be shut out until I come back. I'm quite sure if you walked out you wouldn't know your way around where we are. Just read the book I gave you. You'll start to understand the process of what I have to do to give you a new arm." He caught her chin and lifted her gaze. "When I get back, I'll have a surprise for you."

Netriet watched him leave. For a long time, she just stood still, looking at the rock wall that had opened and then closed behind him. She was caught in her own bemusement, like an animal in a trap. What did she really feel? The tears began to build deep inside, the pressure and moisture slicked over by a layer of rage. She took a deep breath, trying to stop the shaking in her shoulders. It was like being in the Lair again as Philippe's pet. She was stuck and out of control of her own life.

Baal didn't know how leaving her alone like this would make her feel. Otherwise, he wouldn't have done it. He loved her. She was his mate; he had no choice in loving her. But how could a sick animal like him know how to love?

Her mouth fell open at her own train of thought. How could she think such a thing about her own mate? She was filled with the urge to run headlong at the rock wall and see if it would let her through. What did she care if she could get back in or not? Maybe she didn't want to leave it all. She just wanted the choice. Having no choice made her a prisoner.

Resolved to try to leave, regardless of the consequences that came after, she took a step forward. The shadow surged up and slammed her in the stomach like a vicious punch. Netriet doubled over, trying to breathe. The shadow rose up her chest and shoved her backward. She stumbled and landed on the bed. She gasped for air and clutched at her belly as pain vibrated through her. The shadow stretched out, reaching, and sliding throughout her whole body until there wasn't a place she couldn't feel it.

Then as abruptly as the assault started, it stopped. Then the shadow began a different kind of assault. The pain was replaced by a peaceful warmth. It assailed her with euphoria, relaxation, and bliss.

You're in love. You're in love.

"Shut up," Netriet said, unable to put much conviction into her voice. Negativity was proving difficult under the waves of peace the shadow was forcing on her. "Maybe *you're* in love. I'm not so sure."

Don't be stupid. You need to accept there is no you and me. We are one. I'm not going anywhere. If you stop fighting against it, we could merge. Become whole. Then there would be no divide. You wouldn't speak aloud when there's no one there to hear.

The shadow hit her with a surge of love. Netriet felt her heart expand. Maybe she was right. Baal said the darkness was her power, her beauty. Destiny knew better than she did. Didn't it? What did it matter if she gave in? Baal said power was everything. The shadow certainly gave her power, she thought, remembering her abnormal strength when she had attacked Syblee.

That's right, my sweet. That power could be yours all the time. No one could stop you. You could do anything you wanted.

"I don't know. I'll think about it."

Of course you will. You'll think about it, and you'll think about Baal. You're in love.

Everything the shadow was making her feel rolled through her again. "Yes. I'm in love," she whispered, "I'm in love."

The shadow turned her loose. Netriet shook off a moment of dizziness as she stood. She looked around the cave with new eyes. It was mysterious and beautiful. Why would she ever want to leave? It wasn't small and confining. She decided to explore. There was more to the place she could see, aside from the room with the black door she wasn't allowed in…yet.

****

Merick looked down at the old map, candlelight flickering along the overused parchment, casting tiny shadows along the ridges of the folds. His only eyewitness to Netriet's disappearance had said she left with someone through a portal. So she could be anywhere in Regia. He made the assumption she didn't leave with a werewolf. Not many people had the ability or financial means to open portals. Royal and noble vampires would sometimes have an End of the Bridge, but that was a long time ago.

When Merick was in the Crimson Brotherhood, Bridges were scarce and expensive. He doubted that had changed since none ever ended up in the stream of random inventory in the Fair. So she either left with an ogre who opened their own portals at will, one of the few aged wizards left, a vampire noble, or a   *Rune-dy*.

The nasty thought that she had been kidnapped surfaced in his mind again, as it had so many times in the last few hours. Had she been taken as a means of revenge, arranged by the woman Netriet had attacked?

"Merick? Are you in there?" Martia's voice came from the outside of his tent.

"Yeah, come in."

She stepped through the flap. "What are you doing?"

Merick sighed. "I'm planning how I'm going to find Netriet. I wish I knew more. She could be anywhere."

"You don't have to do that. This just arrived for you. There was one for me, too…I'm so sorry." Martia held a sealed letter out to him. His name was written messily on the front.

"What?"

"It's from Netriet. Take it. I'm going back home. If you need company or something to eat, you know where to find us."

Merick took the letter from her hand. She smiled sadly at him and left. He tore it open.

Merick,

I cannot thank you enough for the kindness you showed me or what it meant to me. I'm sorry I didn't say goodbye. I found my destined life mate. His name is Baal, and he's a Rune-dy. So you don't have to worry about my safety. Maybe one day our paths will cross again. I hope you find happiness and the peace you so desperately want. You're a good man. You deserve good things.

I will always remember you.

Netriet

Well that was that, he thought bitterly as he crushed the letter into a ball and threw it into the corner. He blew out his candle and lay down on his cot. How could it hurt this much? How could it hurt this damn much?

Because he loved her. He took a deep breath, feeling the agony that wound around his heart. He loved her. He'd hoped in vain that she would love him back. Whatever she felt for him was now eclipsed by what she felt for her mate.

A desire, long forgotten, long since felt, came to him. He should leave the Fair and go to the coast. Live out the rest of his days in solitude, lulled by the waves of the Crystalline Sea. How long had it been since he'd seen the water? Since he stood on the shore and planned where he'd build a cabin on the cliffs? No one needed him. He could leave.

Merick wanted to sleep off the pain and shut his mind off. He got back up and opened his trunk, where he kept a small store of liquor. He grabbed the best bottle and uncorked it. He took a deep drink and sat back down on his cot.

Who ever heard of a *Rune-dy* having a life mate? That was just sick. Of course, Netriet would have a *Rune-dy* as a life mate. What was it about her? Shit just happened to her constantly. She was a magnet for it.

CHAPTER ELEVEN

A large shelf hid the mouth of the snaking hallway. Netriet found it by accident as she grew more acquainted with Baal's cave. She was looking for something new to read when her bare foot skimmed over the ridges in the stone floor, a perfect semicircle worn from the bottom of the shelf moving back and forth. She looked closer and was amazed she hadn't spotted it before. One side of the tall shelf was ordinary, while light came through the other side. She pushed on the shelf's frame. It swung out slowly, just enough for her to pass through.

The hallway was short. One black door was on her right. She tried it. It was locked. She continued on to the end where there was a pass-through and found the first thing to really delight her in the whole place. It was a spring. The floor dropped away, and water shimmered in the natural basin. Steam danced off the water's surface. Without a second thought, she stripped down and stepped into the hot water. Sighing, she leaned back, letting the water cover her up to her neck. She could get used to this.

Her eyelids drooped as she relaxed. She didn't hear Baal come home. She felt a draft of air and opened her eyes. He was standing there looking down on her. His face was blank, but she could feel something akin to rage from him. He smiled slowly, whatever tension had been around him evaporated.

"So, I see you went snooping around while I was gone?" He began removing his clothes.

She watched him, mesmerized again by his strangely sexual manner and the smooth movements of his long hands. He folded his clothes neatly and sank into the water with her. He grabbed her quickly and jerked her up against him before kissing her roughly. His kiss moved back and forth from gentle, to seductive, and then harsh. Her body responded to him, but then he'd throw her off balance with a shift in his demeanor. This kiss was a punishment, and it showed her how in control he was over her. She longed for his attention, his love, and it seemed like he held them just out of reach.

"You've put your disgusting flesh in *my* water."

"What?" He didn't really just say that, did he?

"I'm just kidding." He eased back from her and splashed her in the face.

"Hey!"

He laughed and splashed her again. She splashed him back. They splashed back and forth, their laughter bouncing off the stone walls. Then Baal grabbed her around the waist and threw her over his shoulder. She squealed, enjoying herself with him, easily for the first time… Then he dropped her in the water. She went fully under, but before she could surface, his hands came down on her, holding her under. She tried to push his hands off. She kicked at his legs. Air expelled from her lungs as she fought him. Water ran into her mouth and nose. In a few short seconds, she was on the verge of passing out. Pressure built in her head, her chest. A terrible ache filled her whole body. Then he let go.

Netriet clung to the side of the pool, coughing. She took three burning gulps of air and turned on him. "Don't ever do that to me again! Why would you do that?"

He reached for her, she jerked away from him.

"I'm sorry. I was just playing…I'm sorry, Netriet. I didn't mean to hurt you. I don't know how to do this."

"Do what?" she demanded.

"I don't know how to be with you the way you need… You make me mad, and you make me feel terrible." He climbed out of the water, grabbed his pile of clothes, and left her.

She stood there in a state of shock and anger.

What are you angry about?

"Really? What am I angry about?"

He said he was sorry. He didn't mean it the way you thought. You should be more considerate of his feelings. You know he's touchy about his things, and you did come in here without asking first. Go to him. Make up. Let it go.

Netriet sighed. She gave herself a few minutes before heading back out into the main room. He had his back to her, looking at something on one of his many shelves. She didn't know how to feel. She hated this odd separation between them. She wanted to please him, so much. There was desperation in her to please him and a deep feeling she never could.

He inhaled sharply as she approached him, his back stiffening. She gently laid her cheek against his back. "You scared me. You were too rough, that's all."

He didn't say anything.

"Please don't shut me out like this, Baal. I want to please you."

"All right. I forgive you."

Netriet waited a beat, and another. Outrage ran up her spine. *He* forgave her? She opened her mouth to spill out her anger, but the shadow clamped her mouth shut. She attempted to jerk out of its grasp. The shadow rolled through her in a wave of calm acceptance she couldn't fight.

He turned to face her, tilted her chin up with his finger, and kissed her gently. Netriet sighed, leaning into him. He took his time, and like his long elegant hands, his lips worked deftly at melting her bones. So cold, strange and exotic. *Hers.*

She soothed herself. They would work it out. They would learn each other. In time, he would become more rounded, and she would become more sharp.

As he kissed her, she thought it would lead to the bed. She thought now would be the time they would be intimate and would really connect emotionally, but no. He pulled away from her and pointed to a silk robe hanging over the back of his desk chair.

"Put that on," he whispered. "It's time for your surprise."

Shivers rose all the way through her as she looked in the mirror. Baal stood behind her, looking over her shoulder. She wore the grey silk robe and nothing else. He combed his long fingers through the length of her hair first, spreading it out over her shoulders before gently reaching around her and taking the lapels of her robe and pulling it open. The fabric slid off her like a breath and pooled at her feet.

"Look closely, Netriet," he whispered. "When you wake up, you will have a new arm. Perfect, balanced, and dangerously strong."

He ran his finger in a circle around and around on the end of her small stump.

"I'm going to cut you open here, and here." He sliced a mock line with his fingernail to show her. "All the scar tissue will be discarded. Look."

He reached behind him and picked up the robotic arm. It was smooth and completely black. The *skin* on the exterior was soft and slightly glossy. Once it was connected, it would look as though she wore a long leather glove. The opening at the arm's shoulder spilled out wires and tentacles.

"I'm scared."

"Don't be, my love. There will be pain when you wake, that's true enough. But there is no chance of infection. This technology is so advanced the arm will merge with your biometrics almost instantly. The machinery will learn you, then become you, as if it were the arm you were born with."

Her fear remained. "Where did it come from?"

Baal smiled. "From another world. One full of living machines. The *Rune-dy* have been familiar with these beings for a very long time. They have supplied us with samples and medical supplies for hundreds of years. I'm very used to working with their material. And I'm a very skilled surgeon, never fear."

Netriet turned to face him. "But I am. It's not that I don't believe you, but...I'm terrified."

"I would never do anything to hurt you or endanger you in any way."

Tears she didn't know she was going to cry welled up in her eyes. "Please, can I have more time to think about it? Just a little more?"

"No, Netriet. Stop being a baby. Don't you care how you're hurting me? Why are you rejecting my gift?"

She looked down, shaking and ashamed. The shadow rose up again, filling her with warm waves of trust and love.

"I'm sorry. I love you, so much. It's just my past...my time with Philippe."

Baal leaned down and pressed a kiss on her neck. Then he looked intently into her eyes and turned her back to face the mirror. He ran his index finger along the lengths of her scars, over and over, teasing and fondling the shadow beneath.

"I know you thought the arm was my surprise, but you were wrong," he whispered seductively in her ear. "In truth, your surprise is for after the surgery. I learned today, after going to Fortress, where Zefyre is on house arrest."

Netriet's eyes widened. The shadow practically writhed with ecstasy, making her feel drunk.

Baal smiled widely at her expression. "That's right, Netriet... *Revenge.* Long, drawn-out, bloody revenge. Once you have your arm, we can go and give her and her traitorous lover, Lush, a taste of their own medicine. But we don't have much time. Forest set the date for their trials. We only have a few days to serve some *real* justice."

"I don't know..."

"Look at yourself, Netriet. Look at what you've become. Look at what she did to you. Remember before all of this tragedy fell on you, before you were arrested, remember how beautiful you were. Remember how Zefyre collared you and sent you to your death, but in reality, you got even worse than that. Remember when people looked at you with envy, not revulsion or pity. And all the while what was Zefyre doing? What has she suffered? What has she lost? Nothing...I think it's time we changed that."

Between Baal and the shadow, it was like when she first came here, and she felt pinned in the middle of the two of them. The shadow moved up, again pulling Netriet under the midnight current and giving her over to the darkest cravings. She was conquered, vanquished, and ravaged by her own evil... And it felt good.

Possessed with a surge of desire, she faced him, reached up, spreading her fingers into his hair, scraping his scalp with her fingernails before fisting her hand and jerking his head back roughly.

His eyes rounded in surprise and pleasure.

"Yes! I want revenge." Her voice came out raw and guttural.

Netriet thrust her mouth onto his painfully. But there was no rough love that came after that, at least none she could remember. The hot and cold sensation she felt from his skin spread over her body, and she became dizzy, then everything went dark.

****

Baal laid Netriet's unconscious body on his desk. He debated lying her on the bed, but the desk was adequately large, had better height for him to work, and the bed wouldn't have been any softer for her anyway. He meticulously laid out his instruments and adjusted the light. Knowing how frightened she was, he'd kept his operating apparatuses hidden from her.

He took a deep breath and regulated his thoughts and emotions. His gaze roamed over her naked frame, and he shook his head at the irony. Maxcarion had been right—going to the Fair had awarded him quite the prize. And he didn't even have to give his loot over to the old man, since Copernicus had killed him. Baal couldn't remember a time he was this happy. Copernicus hadn't even taken much of Maxcarion's treasured possessions.

Baal reclaimed almost everything he'd ever relinquished to the wizard, and he'd gained the collar. Copernicus had been either too distracted or too stupid to take it. Whatever the reason, fate had handed him the trinket he'd so long desired. His power had grown more in one day than years of searching and experimentation had brought him.

Hungry to get on with the night's work, he picked up his scalpel and made his first incision. Netriet's blood spilled out red, streaked with tar-like black. He dabbed at it with a fresh cloth. Efficiently, he made another cut, and then another, until he could see the bones, tendons, and tissue. Fascinated, and practically giddy, he looked closely. The blackness had wrapped threads around her bones and laced intricately through her muscles. He grabbed at one of the dark cords with his thumb and index finger and pulled. It came loose reluctantly at one end.

He smiled and tickled the end with his fingertip. The tentacle moved and curled around his finger like a snake. His eyes rolled back in his head as it moved over his skin, testing his pores.

"Oh, yes," he breathed. "Come inside."

His excitement however, was short lived. Nothing of the dark entity entered him. Whether it couldn't, or wouldn't, he didn't know.

Baal activated the arm, stimulating it out of sleep with a series of coded ticks from a long stylus. The cords protruding from the shoulder roused and began reaching out, attempting to grab ahold of the nearest object. With deft swiftness, he grabbed the largest one and fed it into Netriet's open flesh. In order for the arm to work properly, he had to connect each cable to the right place. The hand jerked, and the fingers began flexing as he connected to Netriet's nervous system. The black threads inside her reached out in welcome to the alien prosthetic, pulling it inside. After his initial direction of placement, the shadow all but took over and finished it off for him.

Baal stood back and watched the rest happen. Her open wound closed around the edges of the new arm. Her flesh fused with the inorganic material. It was beautiful. New black scars emerged at her shoulder, giving the appearance the arm had been sewn on with thick thread.

The jerky movement of the hand relaxed, and the fingers began to move with fluid grace. Then Netriet opened one eye, her dark eye, and looked at him. Her mouth opened, and a voice came whispering out without her moving her lips.

"Come here."

The new arm raised and crooked a finger at him. He moved forward, smirking. The next second he was choking, grabbing desperately at the mechanical arm as the hand closed around his throat. He was yanked forward, face to face. The black tentacle in Netriet's eye filled her iris like a flower opening its petals until the amber was totally replaced with black.

He was on the verge of passing out when the pressure slackened, allowing him to breathe again. He coughed as the hand caressed his cheek gently.

"Beautiful," the voice hissed. "Thank you, lover."

****

Netriet awoke abruptly. There was no pain, none at all. She raised her hands and looked at them side by side. It was nothing like she imagined it would be. It was effortless. Not only did the new limb obey her thoughts without hesitation, she could *feel* it. She ran her natural fingers along the slick dark skin and felt the caress inside it. She tested applying various levels of pressure to the top of the hand. It was just as Baal had said, as if it were the arm she'd been born with.

She jumped up and ran to the mirror wall. Swamped with emotion, she cried. She moved her arms together in unison and wrapped them both around her torso. She was lopsided now only in strength. The robotic arm gave off no heat against her flesh. Nothing else to her appearance had changed. She was no less a monster than before, only now she saw it differently. The darkness was sexy. The darkness was badass. No one had better get in her way, or she'd crush their bones to dust with her alien arm.

She watched Baal come up behind her in the mirror, a proud and gratified smile on his face.

"Thank you. Thank you for making me go through with it."

"It was my pleasure."

She turned around and grabbed him by the collar with both of her hands. He looked slightly afraid.

"I'm all for you testing out your strength, just not on me."

Netriet laughed, and the shadow laughed. For one moment, they were together. She and the shadow were one. One feeling, one heart, one voice.

"So what now?" she asked.

"You've been in recovery sleep for a while. It's almost night. What do you want to do?"

She ran the tip of her nose up the side of his neck, inhaling deeply at the tender spot just behind his ear. Her fangs throbbed and ached. Instead of sinking her incisors into his neck, she placed a gentle kiss and moved her mouth to his ear.

"I want to kill Zefyre."

"Good girl." He kissed her passionately. "I love you." He looked down at her and smiled. "As hot as I think it would be if you ended her life while naked, I think we should get you dressed."

Baal took his time; every movement carried the weight of a ritual. First, he handed her the grey robe she'd worn before her surgery. She slipped it on and sat down at his direction. He combed his fingers through her hair and braided it tightly down the back. She watched as he plucked a small vial off one of his shelves, poured the thick, clear liquid into his hands, and came back to her.

"Stand up. Forest's forensics team is top notch. We need to make sure we leave behind as little physical evidence as possible."

Netriet nodded and held still, closing her eyes as he rubbed the liquid over her hair, face, and down her body. It absorbed quickly, leaving behind a strange sweet scent. He removed his clothes, bound his hair back in a ponytail, and repeated the process of applying the liquid on himself.

She waited while he went into his secret room. He came back out a moment later, carrying an armload of folded clothes and a pair of boots.

"Your size, I believe."

She took the clothes from him. Getting dressed with two hands was a wonderful, sensual experience. The clothes were as black as her scars. He dressed identically.

"And for the final touch…" Baal swung an ebony cape around her shoulders. He took his time fastening it around her neck and pulling up the hood. Then he handed her one long black glove. "Your new arm won't leave any traces, so you only need this one."

He pulled on his cape and gloves. "Are you ready?" he asked.

"You tell me."

"No, are you *ready*?"

It was like contemplating losing her virginity, body raging, a would-be lover poised over her. *Are you ready?* Yes, of course I am. And at the same time, no, never. But why did she feel like a virgin? She'd killed before. What difference was there in this compared to that? She couldn't answer herself, yet she felt a difference. She looked at herself in the mirror again. For a split second, instead of seeing her refection, she saw herself as she had been years ago, back at court. The vision faded as quickly as it had appeared. *What am I?*

Baal began to scowl at her hesitation. His displeasure caused her a mild panic. She'd show him.

"I have killed before, as you well know. When have you killed? And I don't mean your sick butchering experiments at work."

His expression grew introspective. "Hmm…although I delight in my work, technically you're right, this is my first pleasure kill. And I do it for you, my love. Let's go."

He slapped the air with the flat of his hand. A portal opened. He took her hand, and they went through together. They landed in the shadow of a large rock wall. A line of mature trees stood in front of them, and beyond was a house. Built to resemble the elvish style, the whole place reeked of wealth. Warm light behind curtains illuminated the windows against the dark night.

Netriet looked carefully around and listened. There was plenty of noise a ways away. The noise of a city. She took a deep breath, smelling the surroundings. It had been many years since she had been to this city, but she knew the feel and taste of the air. No mistake, they were in Paradigm. And this was Zefyre's house. Netriet's heart rate kicked up. What did she think she was doing here? She couldn't kill anyone. Her heart hammered so fast and hard she couldn't breathe.

She grabbed Baal's arm and pulled him back. His face was right on hers in the dark, his eyes glowing like the coals of a fire.

"What's wrong?" he hissed.

"I can't...I don't want..."

"What the hell is this? There's no backing out now. Now is the time for me to see what you can do."

"I can't do this."

"Stop whining. You've let go of your anger."

"Well, so what if I have?" Netriet demanded in a whisper.

He reached both his hands into her cloak and pinched the skin of her stomach roughly on both sides of her navel. She jolted in surprise and pain, only he didn't let go. He twisted her skin and pinched harder.

"You lost your home, your identity, your arm, your beauty, and almost your life, all because of what that traitor in there did. Come on! Where is your wrath?"

Baal continued to twist. The pain moved to a new level, and something inside her snapped.

Do it, Netriet. Kill her. You've wanted to for so long.

The shadow surged up her spine and took over her body. Cowardly, Netriet sank back. *About time.* She thought. *Have you been waiting for the embossed invitations?*

The shadow laughed. *I was hoping you could handle this on your own, but I can see now you can't. However did you manage to kill Philippe by yourself? Just give in to me. Let's do this together. You'll see what we can be when we're undivided. It will make Baal so hot for us. Let's show him.*

Netriet slapped at Baal's hands with her new arm, knocking them loose easily. She snarled at him. "Don't ever do that again... So are we breaking down the door, or picking the lock?"

Baal smirked. "As you like."

The door splintered around her black fist, blasting inward like an explosion. Netriet watched the effect of her strength. It was so easy. It felt so good, this rush of power. She became high on the heady sensation of being unstoppable.

At the breaking sound of the door, a startled scream came from inside the house. Netriet sauntered into the foyer like a welcome guest. In the living room ahead of her, Zefyre had jumped out of her chair. Lush, who had been sitting as well, reading, looked winded as though someone had punched him in the gut. He stood and faced the intruders.

Netriet turned to Baal and smiled. "He's all yours."

She didn't see the details of Lush's death. Her vision tunneled around Zefyre, everything in the periphery blurred and fragmented. Her memories of the last time she'd seen this face crashed over her. All the fear, and the collar. And she did now, what she couldn't then. She stopped her.

Zefyre cowered before her. "Please...please...don't."

"That's funny. I think those are the exact words I said to you when you collared me."

Zefyre ran. It was like a dream. Objects out of focus, time, and space unnatural and disjointed. They went down on the floor together. Zefyre fought. Striking out and clawing at Netriet. She got her hands around Zefyre's beautiful neck. Their eyes locked. The fear and pain and pleading. The shadow drank it up. Her laughter exploded from Netriet's throat, delighted and maniacal.

Then the cutting began. Long metal fingernails slid out from the black skin of the robotic arm. The shadow was in control of everything. Netriet watched from the background, wishing she could turn away, close her eyes. If nothing else, shut out the laughter. *Stop! Stop the laughter!* But it continued to bubble up her throat.

She cut Zefyre all over, slicing long deep gashes along her face, chest, arms, palms, even the bottoms of her feet. That was where she cut her the deepest. Her blood covered the floor. The shadow toyed with her. Breaking small bones first, snapping them like twigs between her thumbs and index finger. Every little pop made the shadow giddy for more. *What a wonderful sound! More! More!*

Zefyre's screams of pain filled Netriet's ears like white noise. *Stop this,* she thought. *Stop her pain. Just end it now.*

Not yet, my sweet, not yet. She has lots of time left. Let's stand her back up.

Objection roiled inside her. *No! End it, now.*

The shadow ignored her and pulled Zefyre to her feet. Netriet stepped back as Zefyre fell forward, unable to support her own weight on her bleeding, broken feet. The shadow laughed.

A surge went through Netriet's brain. This was it. The moment that would determine everything else for the rest of her life. The second before drowning. A decision to fight, or sink. *No! This is my body! These are my hands!*

She grabbed Zefyre and rolled her face up, putting her again in a chokehold.

She fought against the shadow, trying to regain control of her body. She pulled up from the depths. It was like trying to swim through tar. But with each stroke, her resolve strengthened.

Stop it! The shadow shouted at her.

Netriet pulled harder. The grip on Zefyre loosened slightly.

All right! All right!

Netriet almost had control back, but not fast enough. The shadow moved her hand over Zefyre's throat from one ear to the other, slicing five yawning lines in her flesh with her razor sharp fingernails. One would have been enough to kill her.

Shaking with the effort to come back to herself, now covered in blood, Netriet heard Baal come up behind her.

"Oh, that's messy. I thought you'd still be at it."

"Did you?" she said acidly. "Why are you finished so quickly?"

She looked over her shoulder at him. He shrugged. "It wasn't personal for me. I've never even met the guy before."

Netriet looked back at what she'd done, or at least what she'd allowed to happen. She had to run. It was time to run.

"Wait," Baal said as she started to get up. "Drink her blood first."

"What?"

"Warriors drink the blood of their enemies, Netriet. Drink."

"Never! The blood is dead."

"So?"

"*So?* It's dangerous."

"So are you, my love."

"It's unthinkable. Abhorrent!"

Baal smiled and crossed his arms. "Look at her. Look at what you just did. Is that not abhorrent?"

"Drinking blood of those killed in vengeance is what maniac killers do. It could make me insane."

He laughed. "You mean more insane than you already are?"

When she moved to get up again, he rushed at her, pushing her down onto Zefyre's body. His hand held the back of her neck, forcing her face into the bloody gashes on her throat.

"Drink it!"

Adrenaline and rage pushed her up. She spun on him and backhanded him in the face with her new arm. The force of the blow sent him flying across the room and into the wall. He cracked his head on the floor as he went down. He moaned and rolled over.

"You call this love?"

Before he could get up, Netriet ran. Under the mask of night, her hood hiding her face, she fled the city. She kept to the alleys, blowing past anyone she came across like a midnight breeze. Out of the city, and into the wilds, she looked up into the night sky. She didn't really need her bearings. Her broken heart led the way.

Chapter Twelve

A scuffling noise outside his tent roused Merick from his drunken stupor. He squinted at the flaps. No shadows moved over the fabric. He rubbed his head and rolled over, pulling his cover up to his chin.

"Merick."

He sat up abruptly.

"Netriet?"

Her voice was a broken whisper. "Merick."

He got up, quickly pulling the flaps of his tent open, looking for her. He almost stepped on her. She lay in a heap at his feet, barely conscious. He scooped her up immediately, brought her inside, and laid her on his cot. He lit his bedside candle and gasped, panicked. She was covered in blood. Dry blood streaked her face and hair, and considering the smell, covered all the rest of her as well.

"What has that bastard done to you?"

She moaned, her eyelids fluttering.

"It's okay," he said, feeling it was anything but. "I've got you. You're safe."

"Merick," she sobbed, reaching out for him. "I laughed, Merick! I laughed at her pain."

He didn't understand her. It was then he noticed the arm. He hadn't seen it as she had been all twisted up in her cloak. He held his knee-jerk reaction inside. Was this a miracle or a nightmare?

"Are you hurt?"

"No, not me." She managed, clearly exhausted. "It's not my blood."

"What have you done?"

"Revenge...I took my revenge."

Her lip trembled, and then she began to cry in earnest.

"Let's get you cleaned up. You can eat and rest and then tell me everything."

"Okay," she exhaled.

Merick moved as quickly as he could, thankful it was the dead of night, and no one was milling around. He lit a fire and filled his stone tub, constantly looking over at her, afraid she'd vanish. But Netriet didn't budge, asleep or unconscious, he couldn't tell. When the bath was ready and the fire was hot, he went back to wake her.

She remained stubbornly asleep when he spoke to her and shook her. Fine, if that was how it was going to be. He unfastened the clasp at her neck. He pulled the dark fabric open. The clothes she wore underneath were tight on her body. He examined her hands, pulling the long glove off the one. At first, he thought the other had a glove as well, but when he touched it, he quickly retracted his hand, uncertain what to do. He'd never seen anything like it.

He got a bowl of warm water from the bath and a clean rag and began cleaning the dried blood from her face. Silent tears ran down his cheeks as he removed the traces of death. Netriet. His sweet, screwed up, Netriet. The water on her face began to rouse her. He continued to wash her.

He scrubbed harder at a particularly stubborn spot. The blood wouldn't come off. He re-soaked the rag and tried again. The spot remained. Merick grabbed his candle and brought it closer to her face. No. Not this. This was bad. It wasn't blood on her cheek that wouldn't come off, it was one of her black scars. He remembered this particular scar that marred her beautiful cheek, but it was different. The black of the scar was spreading out under her skin, like a botched, shapeless tattoo.

Merick took a deep shaking breath, his heart pulling tight. She was being taken over.

He hung his head, his eyes sliding out of focus. Grief, failure, and loss fell on him like a heavy blanket.

Her finger traced the line of his tears down his cheek, waking him back to the present. He looked into her questioning eyes. They were more uneven than he had ever seen then. Her strange eye was totally black, none of the warm amber shone through that side. And now the other eye, which had always been clean and bright had a small tentacle of black as well.

Merick remembered what she had said to him about the shadow retreating from him. He pressed his forehead gently against hers, his eyes holding hers.

"Come back to me."

His whispered plea reached straight down into Netriet's heart. The shadow scratched her all over inside as it shrank back. It screamed. Her whole body jerked, and she covered her ears in a pointless reflex to shield herself from the demonic screeching breaking all through her head. Then it stopped.

Merick moved back as Netriet sat up and looked down at herself. She held her hands up to her face, becoming fully lucid for the first time since she fled from Baal. How did she get here? To Merick? She didn't remember. She remembered Zefyre. Seized with self-disgust, she jumped up, pulling at her blood-dried clothes. The fabric ripped in her hands until she stood completely naked.

She spared Merick one quick glance. She'd never seen his eyebrows raise so high before, but she couldn't stop to say anything. She rushed to the bathtub and sank under the water.

Merick watched her. He couldn't help it. He wasn't leering at her. He couldn't think in a carnal way at all at the moment. He watched her scrub herself raw. The black scars all over her body had spread out, just like the one on her cheek. He didn't have any room in his brain to really consider her new, freakish arm. He'd think about that later.

She fought with the base of the tight braid in her hair. After a moment, she looked at him apologetically. Her eyes held no incrimination at the fact that he just stood there, staring at her.

"Do you have anything to cut this loose with?"

His tongue seemed stuck. He just nodded and went to get the dagger he kept under his pillow. He didn't hand it to her but took the end of her braid and cut it free himself. He set the blade aside and unwound her hair. She let him.

When the braid was undone, she sank all the way under the water, working her hands through her hair as she held her breath. The blood washed away. As soon as she surfaced, she was jumping again, as though she couldn't get out of the water fast enough. She looked at the pink water with loathing.

"Drain it."

He nodded, still unable to speak.

She wadded up all of her clothes into a ball and put them into the fire. She watched the flames begin to consume the fabric before turning back to face him. He kept his eyes resolutely locked on hers, trying to ignore that she stood naked in front of him. He couldn't read what was in her eyes. She looked confused. They both held still, caught in a moment that was nothing short of an enigma.

Then she blinked and looked down at her body. Without a word, she strode to the chest at the foot of his bed, opened it, and pulled out the very same shirt she'd worn the first time he'd had her in his tent. She slipped it over her head, its length barely falling past her butt. She sat down and placed her head in her hands.

"I'm sorry...You must hate me."

"What?" he demanded.

"I'm nothing but trouble to you. And you've always been so kind to me... Thank you."

He knelt before her, placing his hands on her knees. "Tell me what happened."

"I killed Zefyre, the elf priestess, tonight. She's the one who took me from prison and collared me. She was a mole in Fortress. She was sending secret information to Philippe. She used me as a sacrificial messenger. I'm sure she thought Philippe would kill me after I delivered my message. Instead, he kept me, like some kind of pet...I was tortured, starved, played with. Before I killed him, he almost took me as his lover...I wasn't supposed to survive the fall. I was supposed to die when I killed him. Somewhere between life and death, I became *this*. A transparent being did this to me. She put the shadow in me."

Netriet swallowed and pinched her eyes shut. "Baal gave me this arm, and with it, the ability to exact my revenge on Zefyre. So, I did." She broke down completely then, her shoulders jerking with sobs. "I laughed, Merick. I laughed as I killed her...I never knew I could do something...so disgusting. So base. I can blame the shadow, but I gave in to her." She hunched over farther. "I struck Baal, and I ran from him. He's cruel and twisted... You'll despise me now. Now you know the truth. Now you know what I'm capable of."

"Who do you think I am, Netriet? Do you think my hands are clean of blood?"

She looked up at him desperately.

"I should have told you about Geanna. I wasn't ready." His eyes went flat as he watched his memories. "I was betrayed by my best friend. We were soldiers. Mindless, order-following drones. He was given the order to kill me and my family, in order to frame the wolves..."

She watched the agony in his eyes and didn't press him for more than he could manage to say aloud.

"It took me years, but when I found him, do you imagine I didn't kill him? Because I did. Mercilessly. I heard the screams of my children with every cry of pain he offered up and every plea for forgiveness. Do you hate me for that?" he challenged.

"No. Why would I?"

"Exactly. The law will call you a criminal, a vigilante. Maybe you went against your real nature. Maybe, in the heat of the moment, you enjoyed inflicting pain a little too much. All right, fine. But you're no monster for killing your killer. Should you have taken the high road and moved past it? Probably. Not that the shadow would have let you."

"Why are you so easy on me?"

He shrugged. "I love you."

His words hit her like a hammer. She frowned. Then she huffed and stood up. "Oh, come on! I'm wrestling with guilt right now as it is, and you've got to lay that on me... Damn it, Merick... I never wanted to hurt you, but I have anyway." She glanced at him and shook her head. "If I wasn't with Baal..."

He stood back up and crossed his arms. "Yeah, tell me about that. Tell me about Baal."

He watched her face and body language closely. She looked almost frightened.

"What do you want to know?"

"Tell me about your first eye contact."

"It was the second day of the bazaar...I was avoiding you. Renee told me you'd had a life mate. I was angry that you hadn't told me, and I was..." She hesitated and blushed.

"You were what?"

She put her hands on her burning cheeks. "Jealous. Gosh, that's so stupid. I was jealous of your memories, knowing no matter what, I could never measure up."

"Hmm...well, I...so, what happened when you saw Baal?"

Her frown set deeper, and she shivered. "It was like dreaming. A pull in my gut. Dizzy. Magnetic. And when he touched me, there was this hot and cold—" She shook her head. "It's addictive, this sensation I get from him. I want more of it."

"You didn't feel lightning in your heart?"

"No," she said slowly, "Nothing like that. He makes me feel off balance, drunk."

"Can you feel his emotions as if they were your own?"

"No."

He reached out and took her hands, ignoring the odd texture of her new one. "I don't think Baal is your life mate. I think it's a trick."

He didn't expect her anger.

"What do you know? Just because you don't understand it. Just because what Baal and I have is not like what you had with Geanna, that doesn't mean it's not real. You're a vampire, and you mated a vampire. I'm a vampire, and I mated an elf. You don't know what that's like."

"Okay, you're right about that. I'm sorry."

"You don't want what we have to be real, so you malign it."

He sighed. "That's true. I don't want it to be real, but my suspicions are valid, nonetheless."

She pulled her hands from his, scrubbed them over her face, and sat back down again. "I'm sorry for getting angry. In truth, I doubt my connection to Baal, too. It scares me. *He* scares me. That's why I snapped at you...it's more like obsession than love. I'm not myself with him. I do things I never would have with anyone else. But then I feel...I can't deny the attraction I have to him, it's like he's *her* mate and not mine." Her shoulders slumped. "I'm so tired. I feel sick."

He sat down next to her and took her natural hand in his. He pulled the sleeve up her forearm to her elbow, exposing all the scars, bleeding their darkness into the skin around them. "How long has this been going on?"

She looked down and grimaced. "It's new. I didn't look this way when I got dressed to go kill Zefyre."

"She's taking over you, Netriet."

"I know. She keeps talking about merging, but it's nothing but a filthy lie. She means to conquer me." Netriet dropped her voice to a whisper. "She almost has. She's getting stronger."

"Is she talking to you now?"

"No. It seems she still hates you. She's sleeping, or something like that. I think taking over me, to kill Zefyre, exhausted her."

"So she hates me, but she loves Baal?"

"Oh, yeah, she loves him all right."

He smiled and raised her hand to his lips. "Be kind enough to humor me. I'd like to think of her as his, and you as mine."

She laid her head on his shoulder. "Oh, Merick, don't…"

"Shh. Don't contradict me. Leave me my illusion, just for tonight."

She placed a soft kiss on his cheek. "All right."

He looked at her in surprise.

"What?" she asked.

He leaned in, pressing his lips on hers. She sighed, falling into the kiss. Warmth enveloped her. Her eyes opened slowly when he pulled back, a triumphant smile on his face.

"He's not your mate. You couldn't have kissed me if he was. Infidelity is impossible to true mates."

"Maybe there's something more to your illusion than I thought… But I need to know for sure."

He squeezed her hand in panic. "Stay with me. Don't go back to him. He's not good."

She laughed humorlessly. "I know he's not good. But he's mine. In some way, fragmented or not, he's mine."

"Look what he's done to you!" He lifted her exposed arm up a few inches. "He makes the shadow stronger."

"And you make it weaker… Touch me, Merick. Do everything you can to make me myself again."

His eyes went so dark. Slowly, he moved off the cot and back into a kneeling position in front of her, his hands resting on her knees. "Do you trust me?"

She looked intently into his eyes. "Above all others, Merick, I trust you."

He grabbed the hem of the shirt at her hips and lifted it off her in one fluid move. "Lay down."

She did. Watching him watch her, a surge of purely feminine pride washed over her as she saw what looking at her did to him. It wasn't like when Baal looked at her. It was normal, natural.

"Are you warm enough?"

She quirked her eyebrow. "What if I'm not, what are you going to do about it?"

He took a deep breath and let it out on a groan. "I'm going to build up the fire… You're going to kill me before the night is done, I'm sure of it."

"What?"

He didn't answer but walked over to the little stove and stoked the flames. She watched him, perplexed. Heat quickly filled the small space. He came back to her side.

"You're beautiful, Netriet."

He started at her feet, his hands moving on her skin. He massaged her. The inky marks around her scars began to fade. The darkness literally pulled away from his touch, shrinking back into the confines of the scars. She watched him work, amazed at his sacrifice. He focused all his energy on restoring her.

There were moments, plenty of them, when his eyes roamed over her, and she could see his resolve crashing to ruins. Then he would close his eyes, take a deep breath, and continue to work on her skin. He worked up her whole body then asked her to turn over, and he repeated the process on her back. She became so relaxed under his touch she was on the verge of falling asleep.

"There. It's done." He sounded tired. "Are you awake?"

"Barely." Her voice was muffled in his pillow. "I think you missed a spot."

"Did I? Where?"

She rolled onto her back, gazing at him serenely. "My face."

He knelt down next to her, touching her face gently.

"I don't think your current method will work on my face."

"Oh? What do you suggest?"

She smiled. "Use your lips, not your hands."

He groaned again, pressing his lips to her temple. Then to her cheek, then her chin. When he reached her neck, he paused. "You're killing me," he whispered.

"You're killing *me* back."

He hovered over her, his mouth an inch from hers. "Just one left."

He kissed her lips. He kissed her as she had never been kissed before. With just a kiss he made her feel safe, loved. When he broke away, the weight and electricity in the air between them was devastating, unbearable. It was there, in their eyes, and they both knew it. She didn't have to leave it up to him, but she did. He had two choices, take her, or retreat. The moment dragged ruthlessly.

He exhaled and moved back from her, showing her plainly the pain and effort it caused him. "I'm afraid if we…there might be some awful repercussions for you, because of your connection to him. And if you walked away in the morning… I'm afraid my heart would break irrevocably."

She pulled the covers up and over herself. "So that's it?"

"You're all done. I've restored you as best I can." He smirked. "I didn't try to do anything for your eye. Want me to stick my finger in it?"

The tension broke as she laughed. "No, thank you, but you could try your tongue."

He laughed as well. "I don't know who would find me licking your eyeball more disgusting, you or me?"

"Let's not find out."

"So what do we do now?"

"I don't know. I have to go back to him. You know that, don't you?"

He shook his head violently. "I don't know that at all. Please, Netriet. Please stay with me. Stay with the Fair. Or we could leave, if you want. Disappear. We could go to the coast. Begin anew. Salvage what's left of our lives and find some peace."

His words sounded so good. The picture he painted in her mind was a soft, beautiful fantasy. A quiet life with a good solid man who loved her, next to the ocean. She closed her eyes. "I wish I could go, Merick. Truly I do."

He sighed and looked out of the tent flaps at the sky. "It's almost morning."

"Why don't you come and lie down with me, just for what remains of the night. Give me a little more peace before I have to leave and sort out my screwed up life."

"I could deny you clothing and keep you prisoner here."

"I suppose you could. But then these walls aren't exactly made of anything soundproof. I'm sure someone would hear me screaming."

"Won't you at least stay the day? Visit with Martia? She's been so worried about you."

She frowned. "Maybe. I'll think about it."

He lay down with her. She dozed off, her head pillowed on his arm, her hand resting on his chest. His heart beat painfully as if the blood-pumping organ knew it was on the verge of cracking in half. If only he could convince her to stay longer, just a little longer. The more time she spent away from that *Rune-dy* the better.

The sounds of the Fair waking began to happen all around them. None of it roused her in the slightest. He didn't want to take his eyes off her for a second, but he could go out, get her some breakfast and some clothes, and be back in a few minutes. No one knew she was there. No one would bother her.

Before he stepped out, he decided when she woke, he would tell her about the night she first came to the Fair. The night Martia had given her a shawl, and he had killed two werewolves to save her life. He would let the words fall from his mouth without filtering them. He'd tell her how she moved him the first time he saw her.

He got the grubby old pack she'd left behind that night, out from where he'd stored it. The patchwork shawl lay folded in the top. He set the pack quietly under the cot and stepped out into the morning.

****

"Netriet…wake up, Netriet."

She opened her eyes, instantly conflicted with guilt, shame, and anger. Baal leaned over her. She looked around for Merick. He wasn't there. Still, his presence wasn't required to confirm the compromising situation she was in. Asleep, naked, in another man's bed.

"How did you find me?"

"I'm your mate. There's nowhere you could go, that I couldn't find you. You live in my heart."

She gazed at him, amazed as a single tear rolled down his cheek.

"How could you do this?"

"I…" She didn't know what to say.

"Come on, let's go home."

She gathered her courage. "I don't know where my home is, Baal. I'm not sure I belong with you."

He touched her on the collarbone. Her eyes rolled back as his touch hit her with a dose of whatever the hell it was she always felt when he touched her.

"Come with me. Let me show you."

The shadow roused from its hiding.

Baal opened a portal and pulled her to her feet. He tucked her into his side, covering her with his cloak. The ground slid out from under her feet. He was the tide. A dangerous, dark, sexy tide.

How could pain offer comfort? Because it was familiar? Why did she long for his affection, chase and beg for it? Because he withheld it? The granules of love and caring he gave her were sweeter because she almost believed him incapable of them?

The portal took them back inside his cave. He shoved her down onto the stone bed. "You want proof? I'm going to give it to you."

The pleasure he gave her broke her down into sharp pieces and erased every doubt she had. He was relentless and kept up his onslaught on her body and senses until she thought she might pass out or die.

****

Baal looked down at Netriet as she tossed and turned beside him. He'd drugged her hard this time. Her eyelids fluttered, and she moaned, the sex hallucination wreaking havoc on her. He smirked, got up, and put his clothes back on. Maybe he should bathe. He'd had to touch her more this time with more of his body than before. He shivered, disgusting. She was so stupid. As if he'd ever defile himself with sex, especially with a creature like her.

Frustrated, he sat back down next to her on the bed and began running his index finger along her longest scar. The darkness throbbed under his touch. This was what he wanted. Whatever this power was that had entered little Netriet should be his. It was wasted on her. The possibilities drove him crazy. What could he become with this power? Could he cut it out of her? That kind of operation would kill her. Not that he cared. He just didn't want to risk damage to the shadow.

He had to keep total control over her now, until he figured out how to extract it. Or he learned what its true origin was. Netriet's memories were not very helpful. She'd been in a death sleep when the shadow came into her. Or was placed there…by Shi? Possibly. Damn. Shi wouldn't tell him anything, let alone help him. He'd have to find a way to persuade her.

 Netriet's true identity had proved stronger than he had originally anticipated. A mistake he wouldn't repeat. But now that she had the new arm, her physical strength was a force to be reckoned with. He wouldn't have given it to her had he known she was still able to fight against the dark entity inside her. He had to neutralize her. But how? He couldn't stand to keep up this lover stuff, and he was too busy for it in any case.

He laughed as the idea of what to do with her hit him. Oh, she was going to be livid when she woke.

He went to the room he'd forbidden her to go into and began to prepare it. He carefully packed up his stolen and illegal items and removed them from the room. Except one very large thing. All these years he'd wondered why he kept it, and what occasion he'd ever have to use it. He checked the hinges and chain, wondering if the metal was strong enough to hold her. Maybe he should just remove the arm. No, as long as the shadow had control of Netriet, it had control of the arm. Then he had another idea that would hold her still and make her obey, no doubt.

****

She felt the pain before she woke up. She was lying on her side, something hard and cold pressing into her flesh, but somehow she felt like she was floating. Her body screamed with agony. She felt dirty in a way she had never experienced before. As though filth had been packed deep down into her pores, over her whole body. The same filth caked the inside of her lungs and clung to her throat.

For a moment, Netriet didn't have the courage to open her eyes. She wanted to touch her face, run her natural hand over her body and make sure it was intact, but she couldn't move her arm. She tried, she was restrained.

She opened her eyes. Her mind rejected what she saw. She sat up a little. Her wrist was chained to a metal bar. A metal bar of a cage. A cage suspended three feet off the floor from a hook in the stone ceiling. She'd been lying naked on the metal mesh of the cage's floor. There was nothing in the room with her, except a stone jar in the corner, emitting a grey light.

The only comfort he'd given her was the fur off the stone bed. This wasn't love. It wasn't even kink. It was monstrous and hateful. And she knew then Merick had been right. Her connection with Baal was fake. It was like being back with Philippe, chained to the wall. Well, Baal would pay, just as Philippe had paid. She'd break this cage open with her new arm, then she'd break him.

As she lifted her black hand to the chain on her wrist, the light glinted off her index finger. Slowly she laid her new hand in her lap and cried, defeated and wishing for death. He'd collared her.

CHAPTER THIRTEEN

Forest listened carefully to Kindel as he described the crime scene at Zefyre's house. She looked over the compiled information on her desk from her team and wished she still had Redge handling this kind of stuff for her. She didn't doubt her team's work. Redge had trained them after all. But his eyes cut through things in an uncanny way. She needed his opinion, but he left her no choice but to go on without it.

"This doesn't look like the work of the insurgents."

Kindel shook his head in agreement. "This looks personal. Or the work of someone crazed. I guess we'll know soon enough. If they strike again... How hard do you want to pursue this? I mean, just between you and me, you were going to sentence Zefyre to death anyway, right?"

Forest sighed and stood up. "Don't prey on my weaknesses, Kindel."

"I'm sorry, that was out of line. It's just that we've lost Redge. And there are new reports of deaths and disappearances by the insurgents every day."

Forest paced a few times behind her desk. "It feels strange... My whole job is strange."

Kindel raised an eyebrow but didn't ask her what she meant.

"Did you know Zefyre was my aunt?"

"No. I didn't...um, I'm sorry?"

Forest snorted. "I'm not trying to be obtuse. I'm just thinking out loud."

"Well, can you save your feminine conundrums for Syrus and speak plain and bluntly to me?"

She rubbed her temple and smirked. "I'm not sure I can manage that today. My mind's all over the place." She paced a few more times. "I'd feel a lot better about everything if Rahaxeris was back... Has the insurgent that was caught at the Onyx Castle been transferred over here yet?"

"Yes. Last night. Are you planning to question him yourself?"

"I'm considering it. Stop looking at me like that. So, I'm not the most skilled interrogator. I still want to see if he'll talk to me. I want to watch him speak. I want to see his eyes and movements. I want to hear from one of them what Copernicus is like."

"Do you want me to send in *the boys* to break him down a bit before you make your attempt?"

Forest pursed her lips. "No. I don't think..."

A knock sounded on the door, and Ena stuck her head in. "Sorry to interrupt. Someone named Merick is out here, says he knows you. I told him you were busy, and he needed to make an appointment, but he insisted it's urgent. Should I send him away?"

"Merick?"

Ena nodded her head.

"No, don't send him away. Just give me a minute."

"Yes, ma'am." Ena closed the door.

"Is Merick an old friend of yours?" Kindel asked.

"More of a friend of a friend. If he doesn't take up much of my time, I'll need you back before lunch. And since I've been blacklisted from the Onyx castle, for my own safety, please send word to Zeren that I need to see him."

Kindel inclined his head and left the office.

For one terrible moment, Forest imagined the only reason Merick would be here to talk to her was because something bad had happened at the Fair. All the time she'd spent at the Fair in the past hadn't matured a real friendship between her and Merick, even though she'd known him as long as she'd known Tek. She didn't have anything against him; they neither gelled nor repelled each other.

As he came in, she immediately noted the desperation in his eyes.

"I'm sorry for coming here like this, Forest. But there's no one else who can help me."

"What's happened? Have the insurgents—"

"No. No, nothing like that."

Forest exhaled, relieved.

"It's Netriet."

"Netriet? I didn't know you knew her. She disappeared from my house well over a year ago. Where is she?"

"I wish I knew... That's why I'm here. I think something terrible has happened to her."

"Why do you think that?"

"She's found her life mate."

"Well, that's wonderful."

"No!" Merick exploded. "It's awful! It like some kind of bogus trick. And I think he's hurt her."

"Life mates don't hurt each other."

"He's a *Rune-dy*! She said his name is Baal."

Forest raised her eyebrows. "Excuse me?"

"I don't even think it's possible. I mean they're like incapable, or eunuchs, or something."

"If that were the case, I wouldn't exist. But I know Baal. He sort of works with me some of the time. He hasn't said a word about finding life mate bliss. But why are you so tied into knots about this? What makes this urgent?"

"She's in danger."

"How?"

Merick looked down and pressed his hands to the sides of his head. "I can't believe I'm doing this..." he muttered.

"Merick, *what*?"

"Netriet killed Zefyre. She confessed it to me, two days ago."

Forest narrowed her eyes at him, trying to process what he said. "It was revenge...Baal must have taken her there... He seemed very interested that I had Zefyre and Lush on house arrest..." Forest crossed her arms over her chest, scrutinizing him closely. "You obviously care about her, Merick. Why have you betrayed her confidence?"

"Because she'll be safer in jail than with *him*. I need help finding her. She was at the Fair, and then she was gone, taken right from under my nose. Taken from my bed."

Forest leaned back in her chair. "Taken from your bed? That's interesting. How are you able to have an affair with a mated woman?"

"It's not really an affair, not technically, but that's exactly what I mean... She's not really mated to him. He's using her for something. It's a trick. He's already operated on her."

"What?" Forest was on her feet. "What do you mean *operated*?"

"She's got this new arm, it's robotic, or something."

Forest cursed under her breath. "When the cat is away, the mice will play."

"Huh?"

"Earth saying. Never mind. All right, I'll help you find her. Not just because she's now a murder suspect, but because I think you're right, and there's more here than what meets the eye. Baal's not going to be that easy to find, wherever he's got her tucked away. *Rune-dy* can open portals at will. Luckily for us, portals can be tracked."

"How?"

"I'm sure my ogre friend, Merhl, can trace it. I'll send for him and meet you at the Fair. Baal took her from your tent?"

"Yeah."

"Then that's where we start."

As soon as Merick left, Forest strapped on her new sword and scabbard. But she needed more than that to feel she had any edge over Baal if it came to violence. Opening the safe in her desk drawer, she pulled out the only gun she'd ever brought into Regia. She still firmly believed guns and Regia should not mix, and she'd contemplated getting rid of it many times. But a tickle in her gut told her she needed every advantage she could give herself. The only reason she didn't want to bring a group with her was her desire to keep Netriet's dignity intact, if she could.

****

Forest and Merick stood back and watched Merhl work. Merick held still, but Forest could feel the waves of unrest rolling off him. Merhl walked in a circle around the tent's room, his hand outstretched, his fingers spread. Merhl combed through the air, making his circle smaller and smaller.

"Ah, there it is," he said. He pulled on the invisible thread and examined it closely, his face dragging in concentration.

"Powerful individual who created this, Forest. No doubt about that. But it's sloppy work. He must have been in a hurry. It's a good thing you brought me here now, the signature is almost gone."

"But you can still trace it, right?" Merick demanded, his composure slipping.

Merhl didn't answer. He continued to look at what they couldn't see, his frown deepening. "I can re-open it, but I have to break the Strata to do it. To catch a stronger thread."

"You have to what?" Forest asked.

Merhl smiled at her. "Don't worry, patching the Strata will be easy when I'm done."

"I've never heard of what you're talking about," Merick said.

"Layers. The layers of our world. You two can't see them or change them. All you can do is travel through them on roads others make for you. Ogres make roads. Ogres see the layers."

Forest smiled at the look on Merick's face. "I know what you're thinking. That you've known many ogres in your life and none have ever said anything like this."

"Yeah," Merick admitted.

"There's no ogre in Regia to match Merhl."

Merhl's mottled copper skin blushed at Forest's compliment. "Are you ready? Once I open it, we won't have much time before it breaks into pieces."

"Wait," Merick said, moving forward. He opened the trunk at the end of his bed and fished out a handful of throwing stars and a wicked-looking dagger. He resumed his place next to Forest, tucking his weapons into his clothing.

Forest watched him with a mixture of amusement and apprehension. "Watch yourself, Merick. I don't want to have to arrest you when this is over."

He returned her gaze defiantly and smirked. "You do what you have to do, and I'll do what I have to do."

Forest shrugged. "All right, Merhl, I'll use my ring to get us back. You don't have to wait around."

"My lady is heading into danger. I am going too."

"Oh, no, Merhl. You don't need to do that. I'm sure that—"

"I'm going, or I won't open anything for you."

"We're wasting time," Merck said through his teeth.

"All right. Fine. Let's get this over with."

Merhl smiled, raising both of his hands to shoulder height. "You might want to cover your ears. Breaking the Strata will be loud."

Forest and Merick covered their ears.

Merhl pressed on the air with palms. Forest could almost see the invisible layer bow in, almost. A ripple went out around his hands. He took a deep breath and drew one fingernail in a long jagged line. Forest and Merick cringed at the sound and pressed their hands harder on their ears. It was like glass scratching. Then Merhl reared back and punched the center of the line he'd just drawn. Terrible high-pitched shattering that simultaneously sounded like screaming filled the tent. They were pushed backward by the gust of wind coming from the transparent hole.

Merhl reached in, grasped something, and pulled it back. He shook the end of the thread and wound it once around his hand. Black smoke erupted from the thread. Merhl unwound it, shook it again, and pulled the portal open.

"Hurry!" he shouted to them.

Forest and Merick charged in, and Merhl followed. It was the first time Forest had run through a portal. The whole thing shook like a rope bridge over a ravine, falling into nothingness right behind their feet. She rolled as she hit the ground. Merick was less fortunate, having Merhl come down on his foot as he tumbled out. The portal shook violently and split into thirds before turning to smoke.

Forest drew her sword, looking at her surroundings. It seemed empty. The three of them moved together, back-to-back without speaking.

"Someone left a while ago," Merhl said quietly. "A portal was opened over there. Maybe an hour ago."

"Then we follow it," Merick said.

"Wait. We search every inch of this place first."

"But there's no one here," Merick argued. "There's nothing but this room."

"You're wrong," Merhl said. "Look closer. This place has many secrets."

"Baal?" Forest called out. "Are you here?" Her voice bounced around the domed cave.

Merick grabbed Forest by the forearm. "Did you hear that?"

"I hear crying," Merhl said. "She's here."

"Netriet!" Merick shouted. "Where are you?"

Her voice was muffled, barely audible. They all moved forward, searching.

"Here!" Merhl called from behind a wall of shelves. "There's a door."

Forest and Merick fell in behind Merhl, their weapons raised as Merhl forced open the black door. Shock didn't begin to cover it. Of all the things any of them imagined they would find, this was so far beyond the pale. Forest could only imagine the level of humiliation Netriet felt.

"Merick," Netriet sobbed as she covered herself with the fur pelt. "You found me."

He ran at the cage and began prying at the door. "It's locked. Help me!" he shouted at Forest and Merhl.

Merhl moved forward, but Forest stood back, her sword raised, keeping watch on the main room from the doorway. The door came open easily under Merhl's hands.

Merick reached in to Netriet, but she shrank back from him, shaking her head, and crying. "I can't. He collared me. I don't know if I can leave the cage. It might kill me."

"What do we do?"

"We can't do anything until we know the parameters of the order he put on the collar."

Merick looked desperately at Merhl. "Can't you do anything?"

Merhl pushed Merick to the side and reached into the cage. Netriet held out her black hand to him and showed him the collar. He ran his long fingers over the stone as it swirled black and grey. "It's engaged. I can't do anything. I could remove it if I were a wizard."

"Then let's cut off that arm," Merick suggested.

Netriet pulled her arm back against her body. "No! I've already lost an arm to that thing. I'm not giving up this one."

"Too many unknowns," Forest said. "Baal might have thought of that. Plus, none of us even knows where the devil that arm came from anyway. It's out of our depth."

"So what do we do?" Merick demanded.

"We wait for the blackguard to return."

"Well, we can unchain her other hand, right?"

"Cruel as it may seem, I think it's best to leave her as she is, in case the order on the collar is affected by that as well," Forest said.

"Come on, I don't think—"

"She's right," Netriet said.

Merick looked at Forest. The pain of leaving Netriet as she was seized in his eyes. "I'm going to kill him, Forest."

"Calm down. We have to get him to remove the collar before anything can befall him. Then, your claim on his life steps on my jurisdiction. And no offense, as passionate as you are, I'm not sure you're up to the challenge of killing Baal."

Merick pulled his shoulders back and sniffed at her. "I guess we'll see, won't we?"

Forest shrugged and turned her attention back to the main room. He was in love. She got it. She just didn't want to see him die. They waited in silence for a while. Merhl moved out of the small space and walked around the main room, looking at things and feeling the air. After a few minutes, Forest noticed both Merick and Netriet staring at her sword.

Forest smiled and answered the questions they hadn't yet asked. "Self-healing glass from the Obsidian Mountain infused with Syrus' power."

"It's beautiful," Netriet said.

"It's scary," Merick added.

"Damn straight," Forest agreed.

A crackling noise alerted them to the portal before it opened. Baal sauntered out of it. His relaxed expression turned to surprise and fear. He turned on his heel and darted back to the portal that still hung open. Merhl brought his hand down over it like a Karate chop, closing it. Baal raised his hand to open another portal, but Merhl grabbed him in a bear hug, pinning his arms to his sides.

Baal began spluttering out questions. "How did you get in here? How dare you? Let me go!"

Forest and Merick came forward. Merick began shouting curses and orders at Baal. Forest thrust her sword under Baal's chin. He observed the blade closely, apprehension filling his face. He looked Forest in the eyes, completely ignoring Merick's shouting.

"What do you think you're doing, Forest?"

"We're here for Netriet, and we're not leaving without her. You're going to remove the collar and unchain her, *fifty shades*."

"Netriet is my mate. What we do in the privacy of our home is our business."

"She's not your mate!" Merick shouted.

Baal looked at Merick and smiled sweetly. "I see you. I can see everything about you, you washed up cripple. When I'm finished with Netriet, you're welcome to what remains of her, not that there will be much, if anything, left."

Merick slammed his elbow into Baal's jaw causing his head to jerk to the side and his chin to tap the edge of Forest's blade. He hissed in pain through gritted teeth as blood gushed from the wound and ran down his neck.

Baal's eyes turned murderously back on Forest. "You'd better hope that doesn't leave a scar."

Netriet whimpered in the background, drawing everybody's attention back on her. Forest pulled her sword back and pointed the tip right under Baal's left eye.

"Here's what's going to happen, Baal. We are all going in there together. You're going to remove the collar, and then we'll be on our way."

"And if I don't? What are you going to do then, Forest?"

Forest smiled. "I'm going to step back and become very interested in a crack on the wall while Merick kills you."

Baal raised one eyebrow and smirked at her. "I'm impressed. This is the first time I've seen you have any of your father's ruthlessness… All right, all right, back your attack dogs off. I'll turn the little wench loose. I've really no use or interest in her anymore."

Merhl didn't let go of Baal. Instead, he carried him into the other room, keeping his arms pinned to his sides.

"I need my hands to remove the collar," Baal said irritably.

"He only needs one," Netriet contradicted.

Merhl dropped Baal to his feet, keeping a firm grasp on his left wrist, while Forest and Merick stood at his sides, both of them holding their blades at the ready. Baal reached and grabbed Netriet's black hand. His eyes quickly darted from side to side, and Forest got a bad feeling in her gut. It was possible he could give the collar the order to kill Netriet.

Still holding her sword with one hand, she pulled out the 9 mm from her waistband, cocked it, and shoved the barrel behind Baal's ear.

"Don't get cute," she warned.

Baal cringed a fraction away from the metal of the gun. He wrapped his hand around the collar and closed his eyes. The metal spikes slid back into the ring with a clink, and Baal pulled the collar off her finger. He quickly tucked the collar into the folds of his robe.

"I don't think so, Baal. Give me that," Forest ordered.

"So now you're going to rob me, too?" His voice grew petulant.

Forest nodded to Merick, who plucked the collar out of Baal's robe. Merhl recaptured Baal's free hand and took him back into the main room. Netriet sighed in relief as she flexed her fingers.

Merick looked at Forest. "Could you give us a minute alone? I'm sure I can handle the chain on her wrist on my own."

She nodded and put her 9 mm back into her waistband. "Just a minute. We need to wrap this up quickly before Baal thinks of something."

Forest walked out of the room and closed the door behind her.

Netriet looked at Merick helplessly. He moved around the back of the cage, put his dagger through a link in the chain, and pried it open. She cradled her arm against her body and whimpered as she rubbed her shoulder. She wrapped the fur snugly around her body. Merick reached into the cage for her, and this time, she fell into his arms. He held her against him and sat down on the floor.

"Thank you," she whispered, her head resting on his shoulder.

For a moment, he couldn't speak. All he could do was hold her and breathe. He had her, and he would never let go of her again, not ever. He wouldn't fail again, no matter what. He would fulfill his promise. He would save her.

"I did what I had to, to find you. I hope one day you will forgive me."

"What do you mean?"

"I gave you up to Forest. I had to. I told her you killed Zefyre. I'm sorry. Maybe there was a better way, but I couldn't see it. I knew you were in trouble. I was desperate."

She touched his cheek gently, shaking her head, tragedy in her eyes. "I understand. It's all right. I trust that Forest will be fair with me. I have to answer for my actions. I forgive you, Merick... Now let's get out of here."

Emerging into the main room, they found Forest and Merhl arguing over what to do with Baal.

"I know how to hold him," Netriet said. "Give me the collar."

"Do you know how to use it?" Merick handed it to her.

She laughed bitterly. "Trust me, there is no one in all of Regia who knows how to work that accursed thing as well as I do."

Forest wasn't comfortable with the situation as the four of them left the cave. Nothing would have made her comfortable except Baal's death. But legally, she couldn't just kill Baal. It was only because he was a *Rune-dy* that she feared he might figure out a way to escape. Her only hope that justice would be done was that Rahaxeris would return soon, and she could turn Baal over to him.

They left Baal the way they had found Netriet. Naked, chained, caged, and collared. And Merhl tacked on the added security of encasing the entire room in a portal that went nowhere.

****

Back in her office, Forest took Netriet's full confession while Merick waited in the waiting room where Ena worked. Forest wrote down Netriet's words exactly as she said them. Every time Netriet broke down, Forest forced herself to remain still, stoic. Since becoming Hailemarris, she had yet to imprison someone she wanted to break the rules for like she did for Netriet. But she wouldn't abuse her power. Upholding the law today was breaking her heart.

Netriet signed the bottom of the parchment and slid it back across the desk to Forest.

"I'm sorry, but I'm going to have to lock you up."

"I know..." Netriet's shoulders hunched, and she looked down. "I'm sorry I ran away from your house...when you took me in. I couldn't stay there. My mind was too feral. I wanted to hurt you... But I want to thank you for what you did. I can't tell you what it meant to me. And I want to thank you now. For rescuing me today... I know you'll be fair when you sentence me."

Forest's heart trembled. She swallowed and again forced herself to be stoic. She strode over to Netriet and grabbed her gently by the arm, urging her to her feet. Her borrowed clothes fit poorly. Forest adjusted her skewed lapel for her, since her hands were bound together.

She touched Netriet's strange new hand. "What does it feel like? Does it hurt?"

"No. There's no pain. It feels natural, as though it has always been mine."

"Did Baal say where it came from?"

"No. He didn't tell me the name of the world. He said it's a place of living machines."

Forest pursed her lips as she touched the black skin. "I don't know yet if it is illegal or not. The surgery certainly was, but that isn't your guilt. I'll try my best to let you keep it."

"Thank you."

"Let's go. I'm going to put you downstairs, where you won't be bothered by any of my other detainees."

Merick jumped up from his seat as they came out. "Where are you taking her?"

Forest's heart jerked in response to the look in his eyes as he beheld Netriet, bound and marching to her fate.

"Netriet is now in the custody of Fortress. She will remain in a cell until her trial."

"Then so will I."

"What?" Forest asked.

"Lock me up, too. I'm staying with her."

Forest shook her head. "Against protocol."

"So arrest me."

"For what?"

"Uh..." He looked around quickly, his eyes settling on a tall vase on a stand in the corner. He looked back at Forest, his eyebrows raised in question.

Forest almost laughed. She shook her head. "Breaking Fortress' property won't really be enough to land you in a cell."

"How about assault?"

Ena, who had been quietly watching the exchange from her desk, stood up, her eyes wide. Merick shook his head at her. "I don't strike women."

As if on cue, Kindel came through the door, looking down at the file in his hands. Merick rushed at him and sucker punched him in the face. The papers in the file flew into the air as Kindel fell backward. He roared in pain and alarm as he scrambled back to his feet.

Merick backed away, his hands in the air. "I'm sorry, thought you were someone else. Too bad there are witnesses. Now, I'm sure I'll be in trouble."

Kindel wiped the trickle of blood coming from his nose, more rattled than hurt, an expression of total discombobulation on his face.

"Kindel, are you going to press charges?" Forest asked mildly.

"I...I don't know..."

"Oh, please press charges, Kindel! Do it for love." Ena gushed, causing his confused expression to quirk further.

"What the hell is going on here?" he demanded.

Forest and Netriet laughed.

"All right, Merick. You're under arrest for assaulting a member of Fortress' council. Come with me."

Forest didn't bother binding Merick's hands. He walked by Netriet's side, his hand protectively on the small of her back. Forest took them to the lowest floor, where she knew it would be quiet. The other subfloors were filled with the current inmates. She closed the iron door behind them and locked it. Then she gestured for Netriet to come close. She reached through the bars with a small knife and cut her hands free.

After returning her knife to her boot, she leaned her forearms on the bars and considered the two people behind them. "I will keep your case on the top of my list, Netriet. I've already decided your trial will be private, due to your unusual circumstances."

"Thank you, Forest."

The well of gratitude in Netriet's voice pushed again at Forest's resolution to be stoic. She took a long look in Netriet's eyes, remembering what she had said about the shadow within her when Forest had taken her in, and what she understood about how it got there. Forest remembered her words so clearly, because they had incriminated Shi. Netriet was a puzzle. A puzzle she must solve if justice was to be brought about.

"Are you okay?"

Netriet nodded as she took Merick's hand.

"I'll check on you tomorrow." Forest turned and left.

She took a deep breath as she climbed the stairs. Stress wove through her chest like a needle and thread. Every step she took upward seemed to have a name. *Step*, Netriet, *step*, Copernicus, *step*, Zefyre, *step*, the *Rune-dy*, *step*, the public's opinion of her, *step*, Redge going rogue, *step*, making sure she didn't neglect her relationship with Syrus, *step*, how long before Baal broke out? Step, step, step… She was making a difference, but was it the one she wanted? Was it enough?

She sat back down at her desk and put her head in her hands. The stress was not dissipating. She couldn't sit still. She needed some physical activity.

Kindel knocked and poked his head around the door "Hey, are you still going to question our captive insurgent today?"

Forest huffed and got to her feet. "Tomorrow." She handed Kindel Netriet's confession. "Put this with Zefyre's murder file. Make a separate file for Lush and list Baal as the main murder suspect."

Kindel opened his mouth, but Forest held up her hand. "He's restrained, for the moment. If Rahaxeris doesn't get back soon, I'm going to be forced to deal with Menjel to bring Baal to justice." Forest shuddered at the thought.

Kindel frowned as he looked at her. "I don't envy your job… We're not behind on any deadlines. Go walk it off, Forest. You look like you're on the edge."

She nodded and strapped her sword on.

"Hold up, just a second," Kindel said. "Can I see it again?"

Forest smiled and pulled her new sword from its carved scabbard.

Kindel gazed at the blade, the same star-struck look on his face as the first time he'd seen it. "Amazing," he murmured.

****

Forest was killing two birds with one stone. That's what she told herself as her feet hit the ground in the Wolf's Wood. She was here to let off some steam, and she was going to find out exactly what Shi had done to Netriet. Her portal dumped her just inside the boundary, and the stench of death filled her nostrils. Forest drew her sword and followed her nose, her mind switching into autopilot. She walked silently through the overgrowth. She was just about to duck out of the Wood when Shi's voice entered her head.

"Forest, you might not want to go any farther."

Fear pooled like acid in her stomach. Not the fear of danger or death to herself, but the fear of pain. Shi warned her not to go forward. She didn't need an explanation, not when she could smell death in the air. Her eyes burned, and her muscles locked down as the fear matured. Her heart beat like a living stone, hard, devastated, and determined. She moved forward, compelled to see what she already knew would hurt her. The pain was already there, waiting in the background to pounce. Just how hard would it hit?

"Careful," Shi warned, as a mother does their child. "I'm sorry."

Forest crossed the line of where Shi couldn't follow. The trees cleared, the afternoon sunlight struck her eyes. She followed the smell toward the shifter colony she grew up in. Her feet moved her forward on the path she'd used countless times as a child. Her mind was caught on a loop, *no, no, no, please, no.*

She jumped and held her sword at the ready as a portal opened next to her. She dropped her guard as Syrus walked out. Their eyes locking, their hearts locking and reading each other. She sheathed her sword and sank into his arms.

"Why are you here?"

"Because you needed me. I could feel it… What's going on?"

She pointed in the direction of the colony. "Do you smell that?"

Syrus looked around, realization of where they were dawning on his face. "Oh no," he breathed. He rubbed her arms bracingly. "I'm here, Forest. We'll do this together."

She nodded, exhaling, and squared her shoulders. They walked to the pain. She held Syrus' hand as though her life depended on it. His hand laced with hers was a tether to her heart. The feel of his pulse in her palm grounded her heart, a steady reminder she was still alive and had a reason to continue to live.

The colony came into view. Forest stopped walking. The pain in the background jumped on her, wrapping its monstrous hands around her lungs. She couldn't breathe. They were dead, all of them, and left out in the open like carrion for birds.

She turned her face into Syrus' chest. For one moment, only one, she let it defeat her. He held her tightly as she cried. Her tears were few. Tears wouldn't avenge.

She wiped her face and continued forward. Their homes had been burned. Her eyes moved over the dead, seeing the struggle in the aftermath, schooling her brain to see the evidence and not their identities, though she knew them all. She hadn't seen them in many years, but they were the makeshift family and friends of her youth. The colony was gone, the people and the place now lived only in her memory. The fact that her mother had died long before this crime gave Forest only a sliver of comfort. Violence flexed through her hands. Tears wouldn't avenge. *She* would.

"Too much... Too far, Syrus. If Copernicus wanted to push my buttons, he's succeeded." Forest shook with rage. "I will not tolerate one more thing. The insurgents will die. All of them, one by one. They have taken too much from Regia, too much from me. I will have my vengeance. And I will empower Regia to have its vengeance as well. Blood will be paid for with blood."

Forest and Syrus surveyed the whole colony, looking for clues and information in the wreckage. The sun began to set over the tops of the trees, throwing them into shadow and cold.

"It's time to go," Syrus said. "You can send a team back in the morning to finish this."

"I can't go yet." Forest's crazy day had exhausted her. "I came here to talk to Shi... It's important. You can head home."

"No. I leave when you do."

As soon as they crossed the boundary into the Wood, Forest found a fallen tree and sat down on the trunk.

Shi materialized in front of them. "You should go home, Forest," she said gently. "You need to rest."

"Tell me what I want to know. What did you do to Netriet?"

Shi heaved a great sigh, not from annoyance, but from the weight of the answer she had to give. "I saved her life. Perhaps I shouldn't have. I meant her no harm. I swear it. I wasn't trying to hurt her, even though she is a vampire. No offense," she added to Syrus. "I didn't think it out before I did it… She was almost dead, broken all on the inside from the fall she took off the mountain. I wanted to save her. She reminded me of you, Forest. Such inner strength, defiant. So, I rebuilt her with the flames of the Heart. Only after I was finished, and she was almost all the way healed, did I consider the issue of the state of the Heart."

"I don't understand," Forest confessed.

"The Heart is dark. I don't think the result of what I did is anything one would wish for… Have you seen her? How is she faring?"

"I arrested her today for murder."

"Oh…" Shi groaned.

"She's half crazy. She told me once there was something inside her that took hold and played her like a puppet… I have to sentence her. How am I supposed to do that? She's as guilty as she is innocent. Is there anything you can do for her, Shi? Can you remove it?"

Shi began pacing. "Maybe… It's worth a try… Yes, I really think I could."

"All right, good. I'll bring her as soon as I can."

Shi moved forward, concern lining her face. She reached out her hand and placed it over Forest's heart. "I'm so sorry for your loss, and that I could do nothing to save the colony, or that I can do nothing to ease the pain you feel now. You really must go and rest for a while."

Forest sagged against Syrus. "Okay, I'll just click my heels together three times." She turned her ring around into her palm and thought of home.

As the portal opened behind them, Shi gave Syrus a hard, meaningful look. "Please, protect her. The threat grows."

When they were gone, Shi continued to pace. She didn't tell Forest about Copernicus, and what he said to her, or that he'd killed Maxcarion, or what everyone believed about the wizards may or may not be true. Shi hoped the information would keep until the next time. Forest couldn't shoulder all of that on top of everything else right now.

CHAPTER FOURTEEN

Copernicus rubbed his chin slowly, over and over, as he contemplated the map on the table. Was the strategy good? Good enough? Or utter folly? He was running out of time to make his move. He glanced at Shreve on the other side of the table. "How did it go today?"

"Everyone's ready. I'm waiting for your orders so I can move them around to their target locations before they strike."

"We need most of our vampires at the Onyx Castle, so the shadow sand isn't an issue. Send three fourths of them to Halussis in the morning, but they are to stay out of the castle until the strike."

"Yes, Father. Am I to go with them?"

"No. It needs to look as though the Onyx Castle is our main target. Chaos and terror must be achieved in Halussis and Paradigm to draw the real players out. Our hit on Fortress must be small and look sloppy. None of our good fighters should be sent there, only the stupid and expendable."

"What about the Lair, Father?"

"Leave it. It doesn't even factor into the strike."

"So, the main goal is Kyhael?" Shreve asked.

Copernicus laughed. "No! Of course not."

"But I thought you wanted the *Rune-dy* more than anything."

"I want *Rahaxeris* more than anything. But I want him alive. Our main target in the strike is here." He pointed on the map, to the Fair. "This is how we get Forest. If I have Forest, I will have Rahaxeris dancing to my tune."

"But what about her mate?" Shreve asked.

Copernicus smiled approvingly. "Yes, indeed. The Obsidian Mountain must be neutralized, with little sister's mage inside it, if we have any hope of snatching her. We'll send every Ogre we have. How many are there?"

"Not many, perhaps half a dozen. They didn't sympathize with our propaganda."

Copernicus backhanded Shreve. "Don't call our message propaganda, boy!"

Shreve wiped the blood from his lip. "Sorry, Father."

"Have you located the wizard Devonte?"

"He's still at Fortress, but since Forest has taken charge, he's been stripped of his titles. He only conforms because she has the backing of the *Rune-dy*. And he's quite old and fading like Maxcarion was."

"We need him. His power coupled with our Ogres should be enough to lock down the Obsidian Mountain."

Copernicus turned from the map and strode outside. The night air was thick. He looked from his new hideout out over the Crystalline Sea. The sharp waves sliced the moonlight into fragments. He took a deep breath, feeling his power through his whole body. "Are we ready for the sea, Shreve?"

"Everything is in place. Am I to go as well?"

"I would prefer you to stay here, but there will be plenty of improvisation when the dust settles from the strike. So, we'll see."

"There's a new recruit I wanted to discus with you. I think he's a spy."

Copernicus raised his eyebrows and smiled. "Really? A spy for whom?"

Shreve hesitated. "I'm not totally sure. He's got military background, despite how he tries to hide it. You should give him a slave mark as soon as possible, Father."

"If you had to guess, would you say he's from Zeren, or Fortress?"

"I think he was a royal soldier."

Copernicus laughed. "Fantastic! Bring him to me in the morning. From now, until the strike, I want him by my side."

****

Forest woke up on a gasp. The bedroom was dark, and she was alone. She threw the covers off and went to the window. There was nothing special about the night, it looked like most nights, but Forest shivered with a nameless premonition. She feared the future. Time was pushing her toward something… something she never wanted to approach or recognize.

She was filled with desperation, a slow burning desperation like a fire ember. An internal demand to know, feel, and hold her love for Syrus in her hands. To drink it down in slow gulps until she choked or drowned. The world was closing in on her like prison bars. Time was burning though the air all around her.

She closed her eyes and sought out Syrus with her heart. She would bring him to her without words. She would make him follow her primal call. *Come here, now!*

A smile curved her lips as she heard him stir from the other end of the house. She faced him as he opened the bedroom door. The light from the hall fell over her and forced her pupils to constrict. Her smile grew. He looked as she knew he would, one eyebrow raised quizzically, a small hopeful smirk around his mouth. She hit him with another blast of come-hither.

His smirk turned into a full smile, "Oh, yeah?"

"Yeah…Close the door behind you."

"Why?"

"Please."

He shrugged and shut the door, closing out the light. By the time he crossed the room and took her in his arms she was crying. She didn't know she would cry. She felt too much. It was breaking her apart.

"Forest?"

She clung to him with all her life. "I feel danger all around me. It never felt so real until right now. I hear time slipping past me with every beat of my heart. A blade hangs over our heads, ready to cut us away from each other…and this love"—she put her hand on her thundering heart—"this is its own happiness and its own sorrow."

"Where does the sorrow come from?"

"From death. There are those who seek my life, who seek yours. What if right now is all we have left?"

"What if it is?" he asked gently, his voice never betraying the yearning and ache in his heart, but she could feel it as sharply as her own pain.

"There is nothing outside this room. This room is the world. Will you burn it down with me?"

Red lightning began snaking and cracking over his hands as he moved them over her skin. He filled her with electricity. It raced and sparked in her blood, bones, and even her very cells. She cried out as he filled her with rollers of red-hot electric rapture. He racked her heart, and wept with her, as they fused body and soul.

****

Rahaxeris gazed blandly at the empty, broken cage. There was always something he had to clean up whenever he returned to Regia from being off world. He reached his hand out and touched the invisible remains of what was obviously Merhl's handiwork. He turned back into the main room of Baal's cave. He sighed, disappointed and annoyed, as he looked over the shelves. Baal had always been full of himself, but Rahaxeris hadn't realized the extent of his narcissism. He was trying to become a god, using experiments, illegal substances, and magical artifacts from other worlds.

Rahaxeris shook his head and made to leave. Baal was the least of his problems. He'd surface on his own without Rahaxeris chasing him down. Baal was only concerned about himself and his own power. Hurting innocents wasn't his goal. That seemed to be Copernicus' job.

Just thinking Copernicus' name made Rahaxeris squirm inside. The ground the Aluka Circle had gained while he was off world was impressive. He had to check his anger toward Menjel for allowing it to happen under his nose. No amount of ire would make Menjel care about the loss of life.

As Rahaxeris came back to the *Rune-dy's* headquarters, his anger grew to such a pitch he had to shut himself in his private chambers. Why was he the only *Rune-dy* who seemed to have a heart or any semblance of a conscience? And just as he was beginning to build some real rapport with Forest, the ugliest skeleton in his closet had to rise up and come back. It had always been a faint possibility Copernicus would come back, one he'd always hoped he'd never have to face. When Forest learned the truth, would he lose her?

CHAPTER FIFTEEN

The windowless cell was dark and overwarm. It smelled of dirt and old stonework. Netriet and Merick were totally alone for two days. Some of the time, Forest brought food to them instead of letting the guard handle it. She'd stay for a little while, asking Netriet questions about the shadow. Aside from that, all those hours, they spent isolated together. They took turns sleeping on the narrow bed. Merick exuded optimism at all times, even though she knew he didn't really feel it. He focused all of his energy on trying to make her laugh or distracting her with stories. And somehow, in the dark belly of a castle, waiting to learn if she would live or die, Netriet found a home, not made of a roof and walls, but the indestructible foundation of Merick's heart.

She could feel the morning dawn, even though she couldn't see it. She knew in her gut this would be the day her fate was decided. Lying on her side, she opened her eyes. Merick sat against the wall beside her, holding her real hand, his head slumped on his chest, dozing. She reached out and gently caressed his cheek.

He roused and rubbed his eyes.

"It's morning. I don't have much time left. I can tell it will be today."

"You don't know that… It could be quite a few more days, weeks even," he argued.

"No. I don't think so. I know it's morning, but it might be late morning, I can't tell. It could be within the hour, minutes even, before they come and take me away."

Merick shook his head. "Netriet, did I tell you about the time me and Tek got drunk and—"

"Shh…" She placed her finger on his lips. "I need to tell you something."

He grimaced. "It really might not be today, you don't know."

She smiled sadly. "Shut up and listen to me."

He turned to face her fully. She sighed, looking into his warm dark eyes, knowing it might be the last time she could fall into them. "I have to tell you goodbye."

His cheeks flushed, his eyebrows raised, and moisture coated his eyes.

"If I am about to die, I want to die believing I was loved. Truly loved for who I am. Even if it's not really true. I want to believe it in my heart. Then I can die in peace. I can die feeling as though my life was not wasted, and I was something other than a monster. That there was good in me, and you could see it, and love me for it."

He brought her natural hand to his lips, a single tear falling on her hand as he kissed it. "Then you can go in peace, Netriet. I love you. It's not a trick or an illusion. You can believe it. Really believe it, because it's the truth...I love you." He pulled her onto his lap and held her. "How can I survive, knowing I failed you?"

"How have you failed me, Merick?"

"I didn't save you. I promised I would."

Deep inside her chest, Netriet could feel the shadow coil and uncoil, but it didn't speak to her anymore.

"You brought me back to myself. You saw me, even when I only felt her. You were my anchor. In my darkest moments, it was you who pulled me back."

"How?"

"Love. Not your love for me. My love for you. My true heart, my real mind, are yours, Merick. So, if this is the end, I have to tell you the words, even though I'm afraid to say them...I'm in love with you."

He buried his face in her hair and clung to her. For a few minutes, they were silent. She could feel his heart hammering, could almost hear it.

"When this is all over and you're freed, will you come with me to the coast, like I asked you before?"

Netriet looked into his eyes and smiled.

"Will you take my mark, and give me one in return? Will you share the rest of your life with me?"

She kissed his mouth. "Of course."

"You're not going to die today," he said firmly. "I know it. You wouldn't be so cruel to leave me alone like this."

"Tell me what our home on the coast will be like."

"Small and humble, because we'll be terribly poor. Buying the land will take almost all of my money. But we'll have a fantastic view of the sea from our windows. The sounds of its waves will lull us to sleep at night and keep our nightmares at bay. We'll have a porch where we can watch the sunset on the water. We'll have peace, Netriet. We'll salvage each other and create a life of quiet."

"And you'll make love to me every night?"

"Every night?" he said in mock horror, making her giggle. "What kind of machine do you think I am?"

Her easy smile fell as the sounds of footfalls came down the hall. She clung to him as tightly as she could.

"It's not over, Netriet." His voice was fierce. "It's not over."

Kindel, flanked by two security ogres, came into view through the bars. "It's time, Netriet. Forest is ready for you."

Merick and Netriet got to their feet. He held her hand.

"I'm going with her," he said fiercely.

"Calm down," Kindel said. "Forest said you were to come, too."

Both Merick's and Netriet's hands were bound before they were escorted upstairs. She could feel her spine as she walked, her lungs expand as she breathed, and her heart moving her blood through her veins. She was aware of every part of her body as she marched to her fate.

Kindel led them to a council chamber. Long curved benches lined the room and rose up the incline of the floors like stacked scales. The voluminous room, designed for many, was empty except for them, Ena, Kindel, and Forest. Forest stood above them, behind a podium, in a black robe, her hair pulled back, her silver and green necklace glinting on her chest.

Netriet's heartrate kicked up at the look on Forest's face. She looked pained and resigned.

I am going to die.

Forest cleared her throat, placing both hands on the podium. "For the crime of murdering Zefyre, Elf Priestess, former high council member of Fortress, and for the crime of assault against the courtier Syblee, and for duplicity… The sentence is death."

A roar of pain erupted from Merick's lungs.

Forest shouted over him. "Death to the entity living inside Netriet, otherwise known as the shadow. The evil being will be removed by Shi, guardian of the Wolf's Wood, who originally placed it inside Netriet to save her life, unknowing the side effect it would have. If Shi is unsuccessful in removing the shadow, a revision will be written on Netriet's sentence, and she shall remain in the custody of Fortress until a solution is found."

Netriet collapsed against Merick. She looked up at Forest, her eyes filled with tears and gratitude. "Thank you."

Forest smiled and blew out a breath. "And since we're here, Merick, you face charges of assault, unless Kindel decides to drop them."

Ena piped up from the corner of the room, "Oh, drop the charges, Kindel."

He smirked at her. "For love, Ena?"

She nodded quickly. Kindel laughed. "All right. I drop the charges."

Kindel unbound Netriet and Merick. Forest came down from her podium. She took off her black robe, folded it over the back of a bench, and tucked her necklace inside her shirt. Her sword was already strapped around her waist.

"Shi is expecting us. She's already told me she's not sure this will work, but she's optimistic." She looked at Kindel. "Are you coming?"

"Do I have a choice?"

"Of course."

"Then, no. In case the extraction doesn't work, I'd rather not be around for Merick to punch me again when you take Netriet back into custody."

Forest chuckled as Kindel walked away. "Okay, are you ready?"

"More than ready," Netriet said eagerly.

Forest turned her ring into her palm and opened a portal to the Wood.

****

The portal closed behind them, and they stood on the beach of the river. Netriet saw the silvery purple water, but she couldn't comprehend or appreciate the beauty around her. She took one breath, the air ramming down her throat, and she couldn't exhale. Her lungs locked up as the shadow rushed through her extremities. The sounds of Forest and Merick talking bounced on her ears, louder, then softer, as if she was underwater, and they spoke to her from above the water. The darkness pushed through her to the surface, caught under her skin, and still it pushed, tearing her open, until all she could hear was her own screaming.

Chapter Sixteen

Merick's eyes were dazzled by the beauty of the Wood. He hadn't been there since his youth. He took a step forward, still holding Netriet's hand, and was jerked backward when she didn't follow. Her hand clamped down on his painfully. He looked back at her, and his heart clutched.

She stood rigid, her face blank, eyes wide but unseeing. The black tentacle in her iris uncoiled, losing its shape, flowing through her eye, filling it until the amber of her iris was drowned completely. The tiny veins in the whites of her eyes turned from red to black. Her other eye began to darken as though bruised. The next second, the shadow was hemorrhaging through it as well, and both her eyes resembled glossy black balls. Before Merick could do anything, or even think, Netriet fell, unconscious to the ground.

Merick cried out in alarm as Shi materialized beside them. Forest knelt on the other side of Netriet and held her head up off the ground. The strangely beautiful ghost reached her long branchy hands down and touched Netriet.

"What's happening to her?" Merick shouted.

Shi gasped and pulled her hands back. "There's no time to do this the way I wanted. We're going to have to improvise."

"What do you—" Merick's question cut short.

The black of Netriet's scars broke out, inky lines bleeding under her skin. Her back arched, and she rose off the ground as if an invisible ogre lifted her up. She hung suspended in the air, her arms shot straight out, palms up, fingers spread, eyes closed, head craned back, and toes pointed.

"Don't," Shi shouted at Merick as he reached for Netriet. "Don't touch her."

"What's happening? What do we do?"

Merick's heart filled his throat at the look on Forest's and Shi's faces. They didn't know. He was losing her. They shouldn't have brought her here.

"What are you waiting for?" Merick shouted at Shi. "Do something!"

"It's too interwoven inside her. I can't just pull it out. I'd have to..." Shi's eyes darted from Merick back to Netriet, hanging there like a marionette.

Netriet began to move, her limbs stayed stiff, but she drifted in the air, her toes scraping lines in the ground.

"Not good," Shi said. "The Heart is trying to reclaim itself."

Merick stumbled as he tried to catch Netriet. He got back to his feet and chased after her. He wrapped his arms around her waist. At his touch, she shattered like stone under a hammer. Her body coiled in, and he dropped to his knees, Netriet in the fetal position in his arms. Her eyes shot open, but it wasn't Netriet looking at him. Her mouth pulled open, and a terrible laugh screeched from her throat.

"I knew you'd kill her, Merick," it hissed.

"Back off," he ordered.

It laughed again. "Too late...too late."

A tremor ripped through her body. An invisible force wrapped around her again and jerked her from his arms. Her body contracted in the air. Then she shook her head and moved her arms, fighting the restraints on her. A terrible scream of pain shot out of her. It wasn't the shadow screaming, it was Netriet. Forest and Merick ran beside her, and Shi faced Netriet and floated backward in front of her. Netriet was dragged faster and faster.

"Cut her!" Shi yelled. "Give it a way out, now! Don't let her reach the flames!"

Forest pulled her sword but looked as apprehensive as Merick felt about using it on Netriet. The sword was too deadly. She sheathed it again and pulled a knife from her boot.

"Here!" Forest, now behind, threw the blade to Merick.

Netriet continued to scream and thrash as the blackness on her skin continued to cover more ground. Gritting his teeth, and heartbroken to have to hurt her, he cut a gash on her forearm. Her blood spurted out, then came the smoke. From the wound, black smoke and oil slithered out, pulled through the air on the same force that had Netriet.

"More!" Shi shouted.

The trees grew thicker. Just beyond them, Merick could see the dark flames of the Heart.

"Shit!" He pushed in front of her, trying to slow her down. "I'm sorry." He cut her on her shoulder, slicing through her shirt. Again came a braid of smoke and oil that flew by his head. He cut the side of her neck, her cheek, and a long line on her chest above her breasts. The darkness ran out from her wounds. She was almost to the flames. She slowed, looking as though she was held aloft by the black cables sliding out of her body.

****

Closed and blind to the world around her, Netriet turned within and faced the shadow.

Why? She cried. *I loved you.*

Netriet had no more words. She looked on the shadow as she paled, turned translucent, then faded away completely. She could feel the slimy ribbons wrapped around her heart slide off and pull away, leaving her breathless.

Some of me will always be with you, Netriet, she whispered as she left. *Just as I have taken a piece of you with me.*

****

Merick, Forest, and Shi huddled around Netriet as she came down, the last wisps of smoke exiting her wounds. Merick held her cradled in his arms. She was unconscious, her head resting against his chest. The wounds he'd given her were already closing. Her scars were almost invisible now, just texture on her skin, the same creamy color as the unscarred parts of her. She was so beautiful and finally, she breathed peacefully.

When Netriet opened her clear, amber eyes, Merick fell harder in love.

She reached up with both her hands and pulled his face down to hers. "She's gone," Netriet whispered. "You saved me. I knew you would."

****

For a while, Netriet stood alone, next to the Heart, looking into the flames. Forest and Merick gave her some space when she told them she needed a few moments.

As she looked at the flames, her mind cleared, and the memories that had gone missing came back. Some of it she wished she still didn't remember, but she would never complain. Her mind was whole, and it was hers alone. She could trust her thoughts were her own.

Netriet felt Shi come up behind her, she turned to face her.

"I'm sorry," Shi said.

"Don't." Netriet was firm. "I've spent a long time hating you...I knew you saved my life, but I didn't really understand."

"I didn't mean you any harm. I thought it was a gift."

Netriet smiled a little and looked over her shoulder at Merick, waiting for her in the distance. "I'm glad I'm alive. So, thank you for that."

Shi followed Netriet's gaze. "He's a good man, a lot like you, with a painful past. He loves you."

"I know. I love him, too...but..."

"But?" Shi pressed.

"He's not my mate. He's already had his mate, she died. But what about me? I don't want anyone but him, but I'm terrified to hurt him. He asked me to share his life. How can I do that when I might have a life mate pop up sometime and take me away from him?"

"I see."

"Do you have the power to see into my future? Is there someone else for me?"

"I don't have that kind of power. I'm sorry. But I can reassure you... You really did die here after killing Philippe. You were not the same person when you woke up, and you're not the same person now. The Netriet of the past may have had a life mate, I don't know. But you're not her. I think it's safe for you to follow your heart. I truly don't believe there will be anyone else for you but Merick."

Netriet gave Shi a hard stare. "Truly?"

"Truly."

****

Baal came out from his hiding place when Forest, Merick, and Netriet left the Wood. He'd watched the whole thing from the shelter of Maxcarion's ruined home. The cloaking enchantment still worked and kept the place hidden from most eyes. Netriet's exorcism had been illuminating. Now he finally had the answer he needed.

Shi materialized in front of him as he made his way to the Heart.

He stopped and crossed his arms over his chest. "Are you finally going to acknowledge me? I've seen you before, from a far, but you've never shown yourself to me. You're not going to stop me. I *will* have the power of the Heart."

"Go ahead and try. I don't care."

Her flippant response irritated him more than anything else she could have said or done.

"So high and mighty. Free to do as you please. No one to answer to... That's about to change. When I come out of the fire, you'll bow to me."

Shi scoffed and moved away from him. "Yeah, I guess we'll see about that, won't we? I don't think you have the stomach for it. You, who are so afraid of scars marring your flawless skin."

He pushed ahead, but her words did stick. The very idea of scars made his stomach turn. Scars meant imperfection. He didn't want to be imperfect. The loss of his finger to the collar was heartbreaking enough. But with this kind of power, who knew what he could do? Perhaps he could grow a new finger, or erase scars. He wouldn't fight the power the way Netriet had.

He needed to move his mind away from thoughts of Netriet. She meant more to him now than she ever had. Now she was top of the list of people he'd kill once his power was realized. She'd signed her own death warrant the second she'd dared collar him. He'd teach her the meaning of pain slowly. So, so slowly.

He took a deep breath as he entered the ring of crystal trees around the flames. He took off his clothes and folded them in a pile. His hand sweat with apprehension around the handle of his surgical scalpel. No half measures. This was his moment of rebirth.

Gritting his teeth, he sliced his forearm, then his chest, and his palm. His heart broke at the sight of his own blood, but he had to do more. He cut his bicep, his shoulder, and his neck. Reaching around awkwardly, he cut a line from his shoulder blade to the base of his spine. Dropping the scalpel, he stepped into the fire. The flames alighted on his wounds and slipped inside. His screaming echoed through the whole wood.

Shi watched, noting everything happening merely for posterity reasons. She knew this wasn't going to go well for him before he did it. Even when she had been alive, a Verdant, blessed by the Heart, never would she have been foolish enough to enter the flames covered in wounds. Maybe she should have told him the method she used on Netriet was nothing like this, or that she had controlled the amount of fire placed inside her. Maybe…

Nah. He wasn't worth saving. So she watched. Maybe the Heart would bless him after all.

The flames continued to pour into him. Blackness spread through his whole body until he looked like a silhouette. He fell forward out of the manifestation and broke apart like a burned up log falling to ashes. Smoke rose off of his dead body and re-entered the flames.

Shi gazed placidly at his remains. Well, so much for a blessing. *Good riddance to the wannabe god.*

****

Netriet sat among the people of the Fair and enjoyed the evening party easily. She wasn't afraid anymore. Everyone was curious about what had happened to her. She discussed it with those who asked, keeping it vague where Baal came into the story. She would have left him out completely, but there had to be an explanation of how she acquired a robotic, alien arm.

Martia stayed by her side like a mother hen the whole evening and shooed people away when she thought they were getting too nosy.

"You look exhausted, dear," Martia said, patting her hand.

"I'm afraid I am. I think I'll turn in."

Martia's eyes filled with tears.

"What's wrong?"

"I'm sad you and Merick are leaving. I'll miss you both. Promise you'll come back and visit us?"

Netriet hugged her. "You couldn't keep us away."

She walked through the ragtag little town to Merick's tent and ducked through the door without hesitating. He was sitting on the cot, sorting through his trunk.

"What are you doing?"

"Getting ready to go. No one will care if I, *we* I mean, leave most of this stuff here. I'm just going through what we should take with us."

Netriet sat next to him and put her head on his shoulder. "Well, I travel light. I literally only have the clothes on my back."

"Will you be ready to go in the morning?"

"If you are." She yawned. "Are you sure you don't want to have our marking ceremony here at the Fair?"

"I don't want to rush."

Netriet was suddenly more awake than she had been a second ago. "What do you mean? Are you having second thoughts?"

"No! Not at all... Damn it, I'm sorry. I never want you to feel insecure, Netriet. I wanted to take you somewhere tomorrow, after we left here. The memorial I made to my dead family is not far... Maybe it's stupid—I just wanted to show you. I wanted to answer any questions you had about my past before you made a commitment to me."

Netriet sat back up, looking intently into his eyes. "Do you want everything, every little detail about my past, Merick?"

He looked thoughtful. "No... So long as it doesn't create a problem for us in the future, I don't care. I know enough...I honestly *don't* want to know details about your time with Baal."

She chuckled. "You know, having my mind all back enlightened me about a few things I didn't realize at the time... Stop cringing, Merick, you'll like this one. He never touched me, sexually."

Merick raised an incredulous eyebrow. "Really?"

"Yup. Not once. I thought he did, but really, I was just drugged."

Netriet snorted as Merick smiled brightly.

"You're right. I like that much better than what my imagination had concocted."

"Anyway, my point was that I know enough too, Merick. I doubt there's anything you could tell me to make me stop loving you... But if you think you've got something, by all means, keep it to yourself. I'm not looking for an out, so don't try to create one for me, unless you want out and are too chickenshit to admit it."

He shook his head and then reached under the cot and pulled out her old pack and placed it on her lap. She was shocked speechless as she gazed at the shawl she thought she'd never see again.

"From the first time I saw you, you mattered to me. Something about you reached deep inside me. When you left and headed back into the woods by yourself, I worried about you. Intuition, I guess. I wanted to protect you, but I also just wanted to be near you again. I didn't even understand how I was feeling at the time. It made me angry…I tracked you easily, and you really didn't go that far anyway. When those werewolves came your way, I didn't hesitate, or question. I just killed them."

He reached into the pack and pulled out one of his old wooden and metal balls and tossed it into the air and caught it again. "I killed strangers I had nothing against, to save your life. I only let you go and didn't try to follow you more because I trusted Forest would keep you safe. I hoped she would bring you back to the Fair…I waited… You didn't come back. You've haunted me ever since then. Every time I closed my eyes I would see your face… Trust me, about you being mine, I have no second thoughts."

She kissed him as hard and as honestly as she could. When she pulled away, he had a mischievous glint in his eyes.

"Well, I have no second thoughts about *you*. That creepy arm though, I'm not so sure about."

Netriet laughed and touched his face, shaking her head. "Through all this darkness, you've been my light. You've made me laugh time and again, in the midst of a nightmare."

****

In the morning, Netriet was surprised by the sendoff the people of the Fair gave them. She was hugged by everyone, and her almost empty pack was filled with presents. All of them, she was told, were for her new home. She watched as Merick embraced Tek and held on. The age and depth of their friendship was obvious to her as they said goodbye.

"Come here, girl," Renee ordered gruffly.

The old woman thrust a fabric-wrapped bundle into her arms. "Just a few things to wear. And one very special something for your marking ceremony. Come back and see us. I'll always give you a special discount."

Netriet giggled as Renee pinched her cheek like she was a baby. By this time, she was fighting back tears. She and Merick had walked toward the gate, down the middle of two lines, and Martia was the last.

She crushed Netriet in a tight hug. "I'll miss you. You're like the daughter I never had."

"You haven't even known me very long."

"As long as you've known Merick, and you're running away with him."

Netriet smiled. "Good point."

"The heart has a mind of its own, and it doesn't give a damn about the brain's logic or timetables. But in case you didn't know, you're very loveable, Netriet."

Netriet held on to her, absorbing her maternal affection. "I promise to come back often."

"I see you found your shawl," Martia said touching the bright fabric tied around Netriet's shoulders. "I have something else for you. Well, it's for both of you really."

She picked up a sack by her feet and handed it to her. Netriet opened the drawstring and looked inside. It was more of Martia's bright patchwork.

"For your bed."

Netriet wiped at the tears as she and Merick turned and looked back at all the people standing behind them, waving, saying goodbye, good luck, and come back soon. And she realized she'd found what she truly wanted: love, acceptance, and family. They waved goodbye and headed out into the world, on a new path, to a new beginning.

Netriet began to question Merick's directional abilities by midday. He tried to reassure her, more than a few times, that he knew exactly where they were going. Finally, he stopped in a thicket and laid his pack on the ground. "I know it doesn't look like much, but this is the memorial I created for my family."

Merick laid his hand on the trunk of a large, beautiful tree. Netriet came closer and looked at the deep gashes in the trunk: a date, names, and a message of undying love.

"I told you, I have no questions, Merick," she said quietly.

"This is for me. Something I have to do that I haven't been able to before. It's time." He reached into his pack and pulled out a rough piece of metal. "This is what remains of my armor. The armor I was wearing the night they died. The rest of it lies buried here, under this tree. I carved this with the edge of this scrap of metal."

Netriet watched as he took the edge to the trunk once more and added a name to the list: Mycale. Then he dug a small hole with the metal and buried it among the roots of the tree.

****

Merick bathed and put on his best clothes as the day began to end. At sunset, the sky came alive with deep jewel colors and moved in long lazy streamers through the clouds as the pale sun sank over the rose-colored water of the sea. He looked at it from the cliffs, listening to the waves and waiting for Netriet to meet him.

He heard her light footfalls and turned around. He was breathless and transfixed. Her pale blonde hair hung soft around her shoulders, and the sea breeze teased the ends in a slow dance. Her dress was the same quilted, amber velvet of the shirt he'd bought for her. It hugged her body and flowed to her ankles. The creamy mesh sleeves hung off her shoulders. But it was her eyes, her wide, clear amber eyes, full of love, that slew him completely.

She looked so serene while his pulse trembled. He was terrified he'd mess this up for her, say the wrong thing, or move too fast. This was a first for him. He and Geanna didn't do this. It wasn't necessary for life mates.

"I...I don't have the words," he managed, cursing himself as he said it. "You look so beautiful. You make me nervous. I can't think with you looking like that."

She smiled easily. "Promise me you'll always remember me the way I look right now."

"I promise," he whispered. The words were redundant to him. He could never forget the way she looked. "I don't know what to say to you," he confessed again.

"You can say what you want to. As much or as little." She took his hands, her face serious. "I am with you...and nothing is going to change that."

That was all she said. It was enough. It was everything.

He pulled her to him, slicing his tongue on his incisor, and sank his blood-coated teeth into her neck. That small amount of his blood sealed itself inside the bite mark, creating a crescent scar on her neck. He kissed the lover's mark and whispered, "Mine, forever."

She copied him, marking the side of his neck. And that was all. Simple, binding, and committed.

They made love under the stars. The roll of the waves lulled them to sleep and chased away the nightmares, as Merick said it would. They slept dreamlessly in each other's arms. The first night of the rest of their lives. And after so much hell, finally, they had peace.

CHAPTER SEVENTEEN

Copernicus awoke before the dawn and went outside. Shreve followed a minute later, rubbing his eyes, and yawning.

"Rahaxeris is back."

"How do you know?" Shreve asked.

"I can feel him. His blood calls to mine. It's time. Time for our family to unite… Prepare everyone. The strike happens today."

****

Forest decided to sleep in. Her week had been long, hard, and odd. She mumbled affection to Syrus as he kissed her goodbye and rolled back into her pillow when he left for work and went back to sleep.

Midmorning sunlight fell on her face through a gap in the curtains. Still only half-lucid, she had the nagging sensation something was wrong. The smell of smoke registered in her sluggish brain. She sat up in bed and sniffed. Then she heard the distant screams. Immediately on her feet, she threw on her clothes at record speed and strapped on her sword as she ran out the front door.

The sounds of fighting, death, and black smoke in the air, slammed into Forest in her garden. The Fair! It would take her too long to run there. She pushed through her garden gate outside of the boundary of her dome of security, turning her ring around in her palm, about to open a portal to the Fair when a stabbing pain in her abdomen buckled her over. She gasped, holding on to her stomach. She could hardly move her body. Her heart thundered in her ears, eclipsing the sounds of her friends dying. Tears ran from her eyes. She had to save her friends. She couldn't move.

What's happening to me?

A rushing sensation ran through her lower abdomen, under her clutching hands. The sound of her pulse in her ears was joined by another pulse, faint and faster. It was the quickening. And she knew, beyond any doubt, she was pregnant.

A voice she recognized came from behind her, barely audible. "I'm sorry, Forest."

"Redge?"

A fabric bag came down over her head. A terrible crack exploded in the back of her head, and all went black.

The End

Sneak Peek of THE LEGENDS OF REGIA-BURNING BRIDGES
The next full-length installment of Tenaya Jayne's spellbinding series. Coming Fall 2015!

Prologue

For thousands of years, the Storytellers came to Regia. An enigmatic people most Regian's considered on the edge of Divinity. The Storytellers traveled not through portals from their homeland, but on channels made of golden light. They never explained why they came, and they never stayed long. No one argued or tried to bar them from coming. They brought with them the ability to reach inside any individual, pull out the cords of their deepest longings, and give it to them, if only for a few moments.

Some called it hallucination, some called it magic, but no matter the name, it was always born of love. Storytellers never worked one on one, but with small groups. Sometimes the *story* began with song. A Storyteller's voice could hypnotize anyone with only a few notes. The experience was different for each person listening. The story spoken, became a visual tapestry, moving and caressing the senses of the listeners. The crowd not only saw but felt the story as if it were their own memory, and in a way, it was. Each person gave something to the Storyteller, an intangible part of themselves, the Storyteller in turn wove it into the story they created.

Storytellers were heart-readers, and the cracks and aches deep inside a person, were as plain to them as the color of the person's eyes. But a story from a Storyteller was not just a quick whisper of wish fulfillment, it moved into the heart and took root, and it brought healing to the listener's mind and spirit. No one had ever had a bad experience with a Storyteller. They could quell anger between enemies, and make the timid brave, because they brought clarity, and clarity gave birth to peace.

However, in Regia's modern times, the Storytellers became fewer and fewer. They stopped coming and no one knew why. On the rare occasion one would come, they would be exhausted within days from the demand for their services, and would leave quickly.

The laws of Illumistice, the Storyteller's world, gave their youth, on the point of maturity, an opportunity to travel the channels for a set period of time, to learn about themselves, and make the decision if they desired to live on another world, or embrace their destiny back home. There was only one stipulation in the law, besides the time limit; once you came home, you could never travel the channels again.

Journey, was a healer of Illumistice. Her time to travel the channels and decide her life path was long over. All of her family and friends remembered their time of travel with fondness and spoke of their experiences often. Journey never said a word about her time. Never.

The glittering light of afternoon warmed her back as she walked up the hill to her plain dwelling. The door slid open for her and closed behind her silently. This was the time of day she took for herself to be alone and look at the map. As a healer, she was always on call, but no disaster could make her give up this precious time of solitude. She would chide herself for being selfish, but her personal incriminations never made any difference to her heart. She had learned long ago, that her heart had altered on her travels and nothing and no one could restore it to its original and proper state.

"Lock," she said aloud to her house. "Privacy mode."

A small chime of compliance let her know she would not be interrupted.

Journey sat on her bed and pulled out her channel map from its hidden place. She wasn't defiant by nature, but she knew full well having possession of this map was illegal for her. The lines on the fabric paper lit up as she unrolled it. Light moved along the channels open to the youth. The channel to Regia hardly ever lit up anymore. Travel to Regia had become more and more unpopular as civil wars there became more frequent. Illumistice governors closed off channels to worlds they deemed unsafe, or would put them on a limited basis only.

This is what Journey did every afternoon. She watched for the channel to Regia to open. The light flickered on and off like a dying light bulb. Her heart jumped. It is against the law to go back, she told herself. Journey's hands shook as she gripped the map. The penalty for this infraction was heavy. Journey grabbed the thread of light and closed her jeweled magenta eyes, breaking the law as she began her travel back to Regia. Back to where her heart lived, back where she left it, to do all she could to save the man who kept it.

Chapter One

Syrus gasped for air as he was jerked from his morning meditation. *Forest.* He stumbled to his feet, trying to breathe. Her heart was screaming for him in terror. He moved to the window and stuck his head out, his lungs desperately reaching for the air. What was happening to Forest?! What was happening to him? Why couldn't he breathe? He managed a gulp of air and choked on it. He had to save them! *Them?* His heart felt the racing of Forest's heart, but behind that, there was something, *someone* else's heart. A child... *His* child!

An invisible force pushed down on him from overhead. His vision began to haze dark. He saw them dimly from the window: a line of ogres, walking steadily towards the mountain, a wizard in the center.

Syrus reached out the window and shot two bolts of lightning, one from each hand, down at the line coming for them. The red lightning hit an invisible wall, fizzling out in sparks against the energy being pushed against the mountain, but he'd broken a small crack.

The wizard looked up; Syrus ducked the acid green smoke shot at him and as he lay close to floor, found he could breathe again.

"Ithiel!" he yelled, praying the master could hear him. "Get down, tell everyone to get down and fight back against the power!"

He crawled to the door. *"Len!"* he shouted for the ogre. "Len, build a portal around the mountain. Push back the force! Everyone, push back! Push back together!"

A Note from Tenaya

Thank you for journeying back to Regia with me! I sincerely hope you enjoyed it! I know that ending was brutal, but BURNING BRIDGES will be out in the Fall. I promise you won't have to wait too long! Your support and encouragement means more to me than I can say. Thank you!

43287476R00122

Made in the USA
Lexington, KY
24 July 2015